SILVER MOON

GREAT NOVELS
OF
EROTIC DOMINATION
AND SUBMISSION

NEW TITLES EVERY MONTH

www.silvermoonbooks.co.uk

TO FIND OUT MORE ABOUT OUR READERS' CLUB WRITE
TO;
SILVER MOON READER SERVICES;
Suite 7, Mayden House,
Long Bennington Business Park,
Newark NG23 5DJ
Tel; 01400 283488

YOU WILL RECEIVE A FREE MAGAZINE OF EXTRACTS
FROM OUR EXTENSIVE RANGE OF EROTIC FICTION
ABSOLUTELY FREE. YOU WILL ALSO HAVE THE CHANCE
TO PURCHASE BOOKS WHICH ARE EXCLUSIVE TO OUR
READERS' CLUB
***
NEW AUTHORS ARE WELCOME
Please send submissions to;
The Editor; Silver Moon books
Suite 7, Long Bennington Business Park
Newark NG23 5DJ

Tel: 01400 283 488

All characters and events depicted are entirely fictitious; any resemblance to anyone living or dead is entirely coincidental

NAKED AMBITION

by

Sean O'Kane

CHAPTER ONE

The training ground was a mass of tanned and sweating, naked, female bodies, dust caked them to the knees as they went through the carefully choreographed moves their trainers were drumming into them – with the aid of their whips if necessary. There were a hundred fit and lithe girls twirling, dodging and feinting, using light training whips that would do no real damage if they struck flesh. The guards and trainers carried the real items however and every now and then the training ground would echo to the report of a lash being delivered to this or that malingerer, or to a girl who had lunged at her opponent and gone off balance when she should have held back and waited for a better opportunity.

The girls were organised into two lines; one line held the light whips, the other one was equipped only with the light plastic shields they would take into the arena with them. Offensive and defensive skills were being honed as the squad was mercilessly driven on under the sun as it neared its zenith.

The Countess Sadia de Groncourt turned from enjoying the view and walked off her balcony and back into the shade of her office as a whistle sounded and the slaves groaned with relief, sinking down to rest for just a few minutes. She knew her trainer in chief – Angel – would be stalking among the prostrate bodies, her riding crop tap-tap-tapping against her thigh as she surveyed the heaving breasts and quivering limbs; looking for any signs of weakness above that which was to be expected.

They were the Girl Squad. The first and only female owned and trained squad in the modern arenas. Some of the guards were male but all the training, dietary and discipline regimes were under hers and Angel's command. They were preparing for their second event which was due to be held in an arena in Indonesia in three weeks and the pressure was on.

They had announced their arrival on the scene with an emphatic win over the Prince of Bakhtar's stable and the world of the arenas was still reeling from the shock.

Sadia smiled at the memory as she took a sun hat from off her marble topped desk and strode downstairs.

It was customary in the finales of the three day events to let the entire squads loose on each other in one climactic spectacle of naked feminine struggle. And once it was clear which squad was winning and points could be awarded accordingly, the male guards would be allowed to enter the fray and take down every last girl in the arena.

In the Bakhtar arena the men had had a tougher than usual job as the female guards and trainers from Sadia's stable had joined the slaves. Even her beloved Angel had stripped off and thrown herself into the fray and Sadia felt a gentle tide of moist warmth at her groin as she recalled her lover's magnificent body, shown on the giant video screens, going down struggling to the end under the tide of hard, muscular male bodies. The only way Angel took any pleasure from sex with men was if the man in question was stronger, fitter and a better fighter than she was. The arenas were about the only places they existed.

Still, she had looked terrific with big, hard lengths of cock stretching her lips – at both ends….

Sternly Sadia brought her thoughts back to the here and now. She had a meeting over at the arena which was now nearing completion and needed Angel to accompany her.

The slaves were being urged back onto their feet as she reached the middle of the training ground. The guards, both men and women moved among the bodies, prodding with their boots and flicking with their whips as the groaning, sweat streaked girls staggered back to their feet.

Angel saw Sadia coming and waved to one of the men.

"Take them for a run and fill the Punishment Pits if any of them look like they're slacking!" she called.

The groans immediately ceased and the slaves faced up to the next task determined that they weren't going to be put in the pits. A line of ten, eight feet deep pits covered by heavy metal grilles set into the ground ran along one edge of the training ground. Any girl put in them immediately became the lowest of the low and the rest of the squad would take every delight in delivering golden showers of scorn throughout the days of her imprisonment.

As Sadia came up to Angel she saw number ninety-seven – a dark haired girl with pretty tip-tilted nipples – was near her. Ninety-seven had been one of the very last to be bought before the successful first event and Sadia had always felt a sentimental fondness for the girl, as if she was some sort of good luck talisman. Angel simply saw her as one of the smartest slaves in the squad, able to think on her feet and be at home in the arena and the squad almost like no other.

Sadia reached out a hand and clicked her fingers. Immediately the slave came to her and settled her feet well apart, putting her hands behind her back.

Like all arena slaves she was clean shaven and Sadia's fingers slid easily into the moist crack, the lips parting and the vaginal entrance accepting its owner's penetration eagerly.

"Let's not keep the president waiting, Angel," she said, ignoring the slave and just letting her fingers idly stir the thick juices of the cunt.

"Okay, but I'd like to get back for the afternoon session. I want to shave another two seconds off the mass log pull times."

Sadia sighed in pleasure but regretfully withdrew her fingers from Ninety-seven's cunt and wiped them on the girl's stomach. To hell with all the paperwork that waited for her attention in the office. She would settle herself on the office balcony with a long cool drink and watch the mass log pull practices. There was a superbly erotic charge to be had from the feeling of power it gave her to watch all one hundred squad slaves, bent beneath the rope which was chained to the great log behind them. Then on a signal from Angel the whips would begin to crack and smack and the line of submissively bent and devoted slaves would sway from side to side as their feet fought for purchase in the loose dirt and dust and then with the whips driving them on relentlessly the line would begin to move forwards, gathering pace as it went.

At the far end of the training ground, the line would be halted while the shackles were moved to the other end of the log and the process would be repeated until Angel was satisfied.

It was a magnificently cruel spectacle. And probably for that reason it was a favourite with the crowds, particularly when the cameras caught close-ups of the lines of sweating, struggling slaves, breasts swinging beneath torsos, shapely thighs straining, backs and buttocks prettily decorated by the lashes. The orgies on the terraces during the mass log pulling races were amongst the wildest that took place during the events.

Sadia and Angel strolled arm in arm through the gate of the stockade that enclosed the training ground and turned towards their arena. The squad of running slaves, with its escort of jeeps, was now no more than a cloud of dust out on the endless scrubland that surrounded the stable. Sadia turned her attention to the building that would soon be at the heart of the whole enterprise. At last the skeletons of scaffolding were coming down and the shape of the arena could be seen properly.

It differed from most of the others that had sprung up in the last few years in that its roof was a closed dome. Mostly the arenas were in warm climates and had open roofs, but here, in Eastern Europe, during the winter it would have to serve as an undercover training area. In the huge car park that stretched out on one side of it, the fleet of luxurious coaches, especially bought in to transport the crowds from their hotels in the city that lay just the other side of the mountains was already ranged. Every vehicle was resplendent in yellow and black livery – the Girl Squad colours. And every vehicle was adorned with a large picture of a naked slavegirl carrying a small shield and whip. Sadia's stable was one of the first to be actively encouraged by the government of the country it existed in and could afford to advertise its presence. As they approached the arena and could hear the hammering coming from within, a line of three black limousines drew up, the green and mauve national flags fluttering proudly on their wings.

Men in dark suits and sunglasses jumped out and stood guard as the president himself emerged from the middle car in time to meet the two women. He was a tall, well-built man with thick black hair, greying at the temples and greased back from his forehead. He bowed formally and kissed their hands.

"My dear Countess and my dear Miss Smythe! What a pleasure it is to greet you again when all is going so well!" He smiled and gestured to the arena. "For our part, three of the hotels are ready now and the other two will be ready in a fortnight's time. And I can see that you are making splendid progress here too."

"That is wonderful news Mr President," Sadia replied. "And indeed, we have just to fit the seating in the arena and complete some odds and ends, then lay the artificial surface for the racing track. As agreed, the arena will have to serve for chariot racing until next year. Then we will add the circus. But we will be ready for our first home fixture on time."

The president beamed at them. "That is all good news! And may I congratulate you on your magnificent win in Bakhtar, it has really placed our little country on the map," he told them as they began to stroll towards the arena.

"Thank you," Sadia said. "However, neither myself nor Miss Smythe here is complacent. The Orange stable we fight in three weeks' time will be going all out to beat us. I'm afraid the rest of the arena world does not share your enthusiasm for the Girl Squad."

"I have complete faith in you!" the president told them and the two women exchanged glances behind his back as they approached the outlying buildings of the arena and the conducted tour began.

The first buildings were unremarkable looking; long, shed-like constructions in the lee of the arena proper, but once entered, they revealed sunken floors divided into many pits by walls built up to ground level and topped by walkways with railings; and there were also wide banks of terraced seating surrounding each pit. A door was let into one wall of each pit to allow competitors to enter and leave – or be carried out through.

These were the pens, where squad members would wrestle, fight with whips or box while the elite solo fighters would have the arena floor to themselves. The crowds liked a chance to get close to the action at times. But as a precaution against anyone getting over-enthusiastic, each pen was roofed in with close mesh, plastic wire.

"There are passages built underground from the holding cells and changing rooms so the slaves can be moved around easily," Angel explained.

Then there were the barracks for the visiting team and their staff quarters and kitchens.

Only once those had been inspected did the party enter the darkness of the tunnel that led from the outside, under the terraces to emerge onto the arena floor.

"Each team's dressing room and changing room opens off this," Angel explained in her clipped, precise, home counties English tones.

As they entered the home team's room, Sadia pointed out where the cameras were and what the 'dressing' consisted of. A sample chariot racer's tack had been left hanging on one peg and she took it down for the men to examine.

"On the day, the butt plug is coated in a special brew that I cook up for the lazy bitches. It keeps their minds focussed on getting to the end of the race just as fast as they can!" Angel told them as the men's big hands explored the crupper strap with its twin shafts and the studded tit straps and the complex bridle. Doubtless they had all seen them used on downloads but the reality was something of a revelation.

She also showed them a studded whip and saw the expressions of respect as they tested the tines and felt the weight of the length of heavy hide.

"It is indeed a tribute to your skills that you get slaves to face each other with these things," the president said.

"Oh it's just a case of them knowing for certain that what Angel will do to them if they don't will be far worse than anything that might happen in the arena if they do!" Sadia explained to general laughter.

Next came a look at the medical provisions – a bench with stirrups at one end and behind it shelves full of liniment, needles, surgical thread, plasters and bandages.

"The Owners' Council has decreed that all stables will provide medical facilities for both teams and have a full time vet on its staff. Ours starts next week," Sadia explained.

The president frowned.

"But isn't that an unnecessary expense? I mean they are just slaves and one can always buy more."

"Angel is inclined to agree with you," Sadia replied, smiling fondly at her trainer and lover. "But I agree with the Council. In the long term it means fitter and stronger stock which will fetch better money at auction. And it also means that more patching up can be done during an event with no lasting damage. So the bitches can be worked harder."

The president smiled and bowed.

"I realise these things are more complicated than they appear. Thank you for explaining."

From the dressing room they trooped out onto the floor of the arena itself.

Down the centre of it stood a long fence and the slaves had been trained in chariot racing down here before the Bakhtar games, when it hadn't mattered that the seating wasn't yet fully ready.

Now, up by the roof, actinic light flared periodically as welding went on and heavy steel clanged and clanked hollowly as the terracing was worked on.

Sadia patiently took the men through every detail that was needed to stage an event and followed that up with a tour of the dungeons – the audience could hire a slave by the hour to play with in the evenings - and the training facilities. They were just in time to see the squad return from its run and watch as ten unfortunates were deemed to not have given their all and were consigned to the Pits for a few days. Then lunch was provided at the house and by mid afternoon, when the sun's ferocity had abated somewhat, the party left.

There was no request made to sample the bodies of the slaves and Sadia made no offer. It simply wasn't needed. That evening, twenty-five of them would be shipped off to the state brothel for a week. It was part of the arrangement. A regular supply of slaves would be available to the president and whoever he wanted to share them with at the brothel, but within the boundaries of the stable itself; training came first.

On the training ground the slaves were allowed water and then rest while the guards took about half an hour to haul out the log by tractor and shackle the rope to it. Then they arranged the two lines of slaves with their wrist cuffs clipped to the rope up by their left or right shoulder – depending on which side of the rope they stood. Angel conducted operations from up on the balcony; there was still some very fine wine left over from lunch so Sadia had persuaded her to stay.

At length, when all had been made ready, she gave them a speech through a loud hailer.

"Listen up you lucky bitches! In three weeks you're going up against a stable that knows you're good! There'll be no element of surprise this time. Right now their stable will be giving them hell so that three days against you lot will be a stroll in the park. I know you're tired. I know you're hurting. And I know you're going to be lashed into setting a record for dragging that bloody log. Want to know how I know? Well I'll tell you. I've given orders that studded whips are going to be used unless the record's broken on the first run. So pull you lazy bitches!"

She blew her whistle and as Sadia came to stand close beside her, the pull got underway.

"Oh, yesss!" Sadia sighed as she watched the guards throw themselves into lashing the last strength out of the slaves. It was hard, cruel beating and she loved it. She reached around Angel and caressed her left breast through the crisp linen of her shirt. Down below, the log had begun to move but there was no let up in the whipping. Some of the slaves were almost lying along the ground, they were hauling so hard. No one had any doubt that Angel meant what she had said. The record had to be broken.

Sadia nuzzled her lover's neck, licking the salt sweat from her skin as she resolutely studied her stop watch.

Slowly the huge log began to slide more easily. Some of the slaves began to cry out in their exertions and their cries mingled with the grunts of effort from the guards as they swung the whips.

"Mmm! Is that not the very heart and soul of absolute power?" Sadia murmured. "All that suffering and effort just to please me and make me rich!"

"Yes, my lady." Angel's eyes never left the watch, even as her mistress' hand slid down to stroke the front of her jodhpurs. Down on the training ground the noise was increasing as the end of the run came in sight. The guards were throwing leather at the slaves as hard as they could and the smacks and cries grew louder and louder.

Angel shivered as Sadia's finger stroked her clitoris through the material of the jodhpurs. The eroticism of power burned through both women and as the leading guard called out the end of the run, Angel's finger clicked off the watch and she turned to kiss her mistress, opening her mouth wide to allow the woman's tongue to penetrate her. But Sadia hadn't lost all control and pulled back after a few seconds.

"Well?" she asked.

Angel glanced down. "Three seconds faster than the old record!" she called out. There was ragged cheering from below.

"Standard whips to be used on the return run!" she added to groans from the slaves who might have hoped for a rest. As people ran to obey her she turned back to her mistress and dropped to her knees, burying her face in Sadia's skirt and holding her to her by her buttocks.

Sadia looked down and stroked her thick blonde hair. "Early to bed tonight. We need to think of more ways to put those bitches through all the seven circles of hell. I don't mean to lose this event!"

They had one of the solo fighters delivered to Sadia's bedroom later on. She was a tall, graceful creature with fair skin and a long, lustrous pony tail of black hair protruding from the back of the thick leather hood that left her only her nose and mouth free. The solo fighters were the aristocrats of the arenas, they usually fought duels and raced in single pony traps or competed in pursuit running. Only in the final spectacular would they be subsumed into the melee.

Angel had broken with tradition by racing them in the six-slave chariots in their first games; a trick she knew wouldn't work twice.

Angel ran her hands over the soft, silky flesh of the slave as she hung over Sadia's bed, her wide-spread ankles shackled to chains hanging from a winch. She let her fingers trail across the swells of the buttocks and the breasts and the taut length of the thighs. She was kneeling naked on the bed behind the girl and pressed her own breasts against the slave's buttocks, rubbing the nipples and sighing in pleasure, at the same time as she felt the heat from the candle. Below her the slave gave a soft gasp as the candle, which was stuck into her cunt dripped a little more wax onto her. The flickering light it gave out was the only illumination and by it Angel could see Sadia standing by the window, a warm night wind was blowing the long lace curtain against her nakedness and she could see every curve of her adored lover's body.

She was gazing down at the training ground and the stockade, patrolled now by two or three sleepy guards. The barracks were dark and silent. But Angel knew the pressures of running such a large enterprise didn't stop with the setting of the sun, and she knew that in the morning she was going to have to add to Sadia's problems. There had been a couple of phone calls late on in the day. But for now....

She got off the bed and went to stand close behind her lover, pressing her breasts against Sadia's back and running her hands down her smooth flanks, then diving them forwards to run her fingers through the soft fleece of pubes at her delta, still wet from Angel's tongue and her own discharge at orgasm.

Angel nuzzled Sadia's neck. "Come back to bed and whip this bitch with me," she whispered.

Smiling, Sadia allowed herself to be led back and took up a long tailed flogger while Angel snuffed out the candle and tore it from the mound of wax it had built up along the slave's labia, before tearing off the mound itself.

"I bet the silly bitch won't thank me for having saved her from being waxed by the grooms for a few days," she said as she stood back, the slave's body still trembling in the aftermath of the unexpected pain.

Sadia laughed as she swung the whip and Angel was happy to see her relax. The slave's body convulsed and curled in shock again but then Angel reached out and steadied it by grasping the erect nipples so that Sadia should have a steady target.

The two dominants enjoyed the therapeutic hiss and smack of the whip as it landed between the long thighs, time and again in a steady rhythm that eventually brought a shuddering groan of release from the slave. Sadia stopped the beating and ran the tails through her hand while Angel leaned in and lapped at the puffy labia, savouring the juices the whip had fetched forth and sucking at the hardened clitoris, standing eagerly to attention and demanding more punishment.

Sadia came to kneel behind the slave and leaned forward to kiss Angel, tasting the slave from within her mouth.

"Take her down," she whispered thickly.

Angel leaned over to the head of the bed and took the control unit, pressing the control to lower the chains. Motors whined and the suspended body was gently delivered to the bed; Sadia guiding it down to lie on its back, hands still secured under it.

While Angel unshackled the slave's ankles, Sadia was buckling on the thickest strap- on in their extensive collection and while she tidied away the chains by raising them again, Sadia threw herself onto the prone slave and began fucking her in a frenzy of urgency, grinding her clit against the hard rubber as she did so.

Angel took something from the bedside cabinet beside her and knelt above the bucking bodies on the bed; the slave was thrusting back at her owner as hard as her owner could ram into her. Angel knelt facing Sadia's bottom and leaning forward, she parted the cheeks and located the pre-lubed head of the solid glass dildo at Sadia's anus, then she pushed and grinned as the first ball disappeared easily into the rectum, causing Sadia to yell and buck with even greater fervour. She pushed again and the second, slightly larger ball was suctioned smoothly in. Sadia was grunting now and her thrusts became violent slams. The slave began to moan urgently. Angel pushed and twisted once more and the final two balls entered Sadia, leaving Angel enough to hold onto while she gently eased the thing in and out while Sadia bucked with ever greater frenzy.

At last both bodies reached a crescendo of slamming against each other and slave and owner locked into the equality of orgasm. Then Sadia slumped forwards and moaned feebly as Angel extracted the dildo before lying down beside the two fragrant and sweat-streaked bodies. Sadia's face was resting on one of the slave's heaving breasts. She opened her eyes and grinned at Angel.

"Fuck it from the back while I wax its tits," she whispered.

It took only a few moments to unbuckle the strap-on from Sadia and buckle it onto Angel, the thick shaft glistening and scented with the slave's discharge. Then the slave was knelt up and Angel knelt behind her, holding her by the shoulders while Sadia whipped the breasts until she judged they were properly sensitised for the wax. Bending the pliant body away from her with one hand, Angel located the head of the dildo at the slave's anus and then began a steady thrust. The practised orifice put up relatively little resistance and soon Angel could hold the slave tight against her and rub her own clit on the shaft as it steadily buggered the warm, soft body she held tightly against her, cupping the soft breasts carefully, so as not to get the wax on her fingers.

Sadia knelt in front of them and as Angel looked over the slave's shoulder, tipped the candles slightly so that blobs of wax could land first on one breast and then on the other. The body lurched against Angel as the heat came as a shock to the hooded slave. And she could feel the anguish as the heat intensified for a few seconds before it dissipated. And she could feel the tension in the body as it waited for the next bolt of bright pain to explode into its darkness.

Once she was sure that the slave was going to behave herself and obediently thrust her breasts forwards for Sadia, Angel let her hands run down to the beginning of the cleft of her sex and find the clitoris. It was still erect and hard from its whipping and the subsequent orgasms. Angel gently rubbed it as she ground herself against the dildo and pumped it into the slave's backside. She began to moan even as Angel felt the first stirrings of her own orgasm.

Sadia increased the tempo of the waxing. The slave jerked and trembled against Angel, who rubbed the girl's clit relentlessly and harshly.

Hot wax hit both nipples at once and the slave climaxed just as Angel found her own release and the room echoed once more to the combined shrieks of orgasm.

CHAPTER TWO

Carlo Suarez put the phone down and smiled broadly.
"I could almost feel sorry for milady's Girl Squad," he said.

Brian Holden looked up from downloading one of the CSL slave's latest performance stats onto the reader that would update her implanted chip.

"Why?" he asked, a small buzz of alarm running through him. He hadn't told anyone that Amelia – his ex sub and onetime CSL groom - had run away to become a slave in that stable.

"That was Craig Maddox, the Orange trainer. They want to hire in Blondie, Ayesha, Beast, El Tigre, Ox, Trouble, Fiji and Jet for the next show – which is against Sadia's stable."

Tony, the third of the CSL trainers let out a low whistle. "That's big money! I mean seriously big money!"

For a moment Carlo looked thoughtful. "You're right," he said. "And I wonder if they've got it all themselves."

"You mean someone's lending them some, just to put Sadia's lot in their place?" Brian asked.

"Could be. They're all big impact players. Okay, so Blondie, Jet and Ayesha can run as well as any and fight better than pretty well anybody, but mainly they've gone for whip fodder," Carlo said thoughtfully. "Beat the crap out of them over the first two days and let the third take its course? That could be the tactic. Oh well, not our problem. And I can feel that new Ferrari coming on!" he gave his infectious grin and stepped out of the office into the stableyard to take two of CSL's other slaves up to the indoor arena for training.

CSL was the only stable on the circuit that didn't have its own proper arena. Instead it specialised in producing high class stock for other stables to hire in for specific reasons. It had two of the best slaves in the world in Blondie and Ayesha and the cost of hiring them both plus another six was astronomical.

Brian thought that Carlo was probably right. Several of the owners must have combined resources in an attempt to avenge the defeat of the Bakhtar stable in the Girl Squad's shock debut. The Countess's Girl Squad – the one and only female run stable on the circuit - was going to get pounded. In his mind's eye he saw Amelia, bloodied but defiant, struggling to her feet again and again, before going down to certain defeat. He dearly loved how she looked after a good session of punishment, but he wasn't sure he was happy with the picture his imagination was cooking up.

Sadia put her breakfast coffee cup down and couldn't prevent it rattling slightly against the saucer as her hand shook.

"How did you find this out?" she asked.

"I make sure I keep my ear to the ground. I'm afraid there's no mistake. Someone's ploughed in a fortune to make sure our bitches get trashed. With some of the talent they've hired in to put alongside a decent enough squad anyway, we might have to sell some of our livestock afterwards. They might be that badly damaged!"

Sadia rubbed her forehead with one hand and irritably waved away the guard who was delivering a morning beating to a naked slave tied to a whipping post beside them. He bowed and left, leaving the delightfully marked squad girl gasping and shuddering in the wake of an orgasm.

"And I'm afraid it gets worse," Angel went on reluctantly.

"Go on," Sadia looked up, her face set and determined.

"We've got twenty fewer slaves than most of the stables, so we've got no spares or substitutes. That means that all our stock are going to be knocked to hell and back after these games and then they've got to come back here and face another games in only a few weeks' time. They'll get creamed all over again! And if there is a consortium out to get us, there's nothing to stop them hiring in CSL stock for those games as well!"

"They're out to destroy us," Sadia said flatly.

"Yes."

"What do you suggest......oh take that bitch away!" Sadia snapped and a guard stepped forwards to release the beaten slave from her post, against which she had been trying to rub herself to orgasm again.

"I need those extra twenty slaves! I told you we were too tightly stretched! Okay we got away with it once, but that's all. They'll pound us at the Orange team's arena and then......well I don't want to think about what they'll do to us here!"

"I told you, Eric won't stump up for any more!"

"Eric will stump up for anything you want if you fuck him!" Angel retorted.

For a moment there was a tense silence between the two women.

"Anything else?" Sadia asked coldly.

Angel sighed. She hadn't wanted it to come out like that, but there just was no alternative. Eric, their banker, was besotted with Sadia. And if opening her legs for him was the only way they could get more slaves out of him, then Angel would hold her down for him. Sadia had just realised that and the realisation had come as a nasty shock.

Angel took a deep breath and went on. "I think the president ought to suddenly discover that there is a serious labour dispute on the arena site, which could set back the date of our first home fixture by weeks or even months."

"He isn't going to like that."

"He'll like it less if the stable has to close, or becomes a laughing stock." She paused for a moment. "If necessary I'll fuck him."

There was a further silence and then Sadia put her head back and laughed.

"Very well then," she said when the laughter had died. "We fight back with our cunts first and with our bitches second! But no; I will fuck the president as well. Your job is to get our existing stock into the best shape you can. An honourable defeat is better than an embarrassing walkover."

Angel relaxed and high fived her employer and lover across the table.

"Seriously, I need at least twenty more," Angel said as they rose from the table.

"And you shall have them," Sadia assured her, linking arms with her. "And that damn president doesn't know how lucky he's going to get!"

Angel stopped suddenly, frowning in thought. "How much have we got in the kitty right now?" she asked.

"Some. Why?"

"They haven't hired in the whole of CSL, so why don't we see what we can afford? As you said, we'll probably still get beaten, but we might avoid getting massacred."

By late that afternoon Sadia was ensconced in the president's private office. With them was the general secretary of the country's construction, transport and municipal workers. In effect he was the second most influential man in the country. Some said he was considerably more than that.

For the moment however, he was content to stand by one of the tall windows and allow the president and the countess to talk.

"I cannot pretend that you do not disappoint me, Countess," he was saying having listened to Sadia's update. "However, I can see the logic in having a delay before the first event at our own arena. How about you, Leonid?"

The union man turned from admiring the view of the state brothel and its magnificent grounds, in which two or three pony girls were being drilled on the lunge rein.

"Indeed. It is disappointing," he said. "But unavoidable. Better to wait and improve the odds on being successful than to rush in and look foolish. However........"

"Yes," the president broke in, sitting back and steepling his fingers beneath his chin. "However, Sadia, there is a lot of money at stake. Leonid's men will have to be paid while they are on strike."

Sadia nodded. She and Angel had been through this before she had left. "For the first two home games; win or lose, we will pay 50 per cent more to the government than originally agreed."

The men both nodded but then the union boss spoke again. "I am afraid I can foresee some restlessness and maybe even civil disorder towards the end of the two months you are asking for. Many of the men have been looking forward to watching the games; they have paid heavy taxes to fund the arena........." Again he left his sentence hanging.

Sadia nodded again. This had also been anticipated. "For the final fortnight before the games, we will allow a fixed number of men access to my bitches each day. It will be for sex only, however. They must understand that anything else is out of the question that close to an event."

The two men looked at each other.

"I can sell that, provided the strikers get front row seats," the general secretary said.

"Agreed," Sadia replied.

The president smiled and relaxed. "Good, now that that's settled, there's just the matter of ourselves. Our disappointment is deeply felt, my dear lady, and I'm afraid it must be addressed."

Sadia stood up and shrugged off her jacket, then began to unbutton her blouse. The two men removed their jackets. When she had taken her bra off, and her large, pale breasts with their wide areolas and pinkly erect nipples swung free on her chest, the president reached for them, his big hands clasping and clawing harshly into the soft flesh, making it bulge through the gaps between his fingers.

He spent a few moments just feeling the succulence of her body before he stepped back.

"Get your skirt off," he said curtly. "You'll take me first and then Leonid. Whichever hole we choose."

Sadia nodded as she unzipped the skirt and began to push it down her thighs, she could hear the thickness of excitement in the president's voice and knew that if she just took a couple of quick ones over the desk, then she would have bought time for the Girl Squad to fully measure up to the requirements of the arena circuit.

"And then my bodyguards," Leonid added as he came closer, smiling grimly.

Sadia turned to the president in alarm.

"Good point, Leonid," he said, coming closer. "Those boys were really looking forward to the first games. Mine were too!"

She hadn't bothered with wearing knickers and was now standing in only her high heeled shoes. Before these large and clothed men, she began to feel uncomfortably vulnerable. She wished she had brought Angel with her – or even let her take the gang bang that was so surely coming – but she banished the thought. Angel had some real problems with men; she didn't. She could take cock quite happily, it was just that this afternoon it looked as though she was going to take a lot more cock than she had for a very long time. She had passed the bodyguards in the corridor outside, some fifteen or sixteen, big men.

"Your choice, Mr President," the general secretary offered with a sardonic smile.

"Thank you, Leonid. I shall take the cunt I think. I hope that won't inhibit your choice of hole?"

"No. I am quite happy with the arse and after that I don't think the boys will be bothered about her being a bit sloppy."

Sadia had been backed up against the desk by this time and could feel the edge digging into her buttocks. All her life she had been a sexual predator, desired by others and using it to her advantage. They came as grateful supplicants when she deigned to allow them use of her body. Never had she been talked about as though she was one of her own slaves. She knew slaves' cunts got wet when they were abused in this way but her own felt ominously dry. It was time to take a lead and make sure she didn't suffer any more than she had to. She parted her legs and put her hands between them. One rubbed frantically at her clitoris, the other delved up inside her to try and stimulate her inner tissues.

The men began to strip off their jackets as they watched her with blatant lust. Sadia saw that her action had instantly hardened them into full erection and the sight came to her rescue. She felt herself begin to respond and knew that she could cope easily enough from then on.

The president had her from behind, bent over the desk. His big hands mauled her buttocks and hips as he thrust in and out. It was the most impersonal and somehow the most scornful fuck she had ever had. For once she felt worthless and shamed by the sperm that oozed from her as he withdrew. She bit her lip however and determined to endure. Her stable's future was depending on this afternoon's work, but when she got back, she would make one of her slaves' life a living hell. She felt the men change places behind her and then the secretary's fingers were scooping out the juices from her cunt and spreading them around her anus. Then she felt him lodge himself at that entrance and begin to push. That wasn't so bad. She was partial to anal penetration by cock or dildo and she even managed to enjoy the buggery a little bit. While she was being taken however, she could hear the president summoning the bodyguards and explaining the forfeit she was paying. She heard them approach the desk as she tried to concentrate on the pleasant sensations in her rectum and the piles of paper in front of her eyes. But suddenly her hair was grabbed and she was swung round - even while the secretary continued to bugger her – until she was across a corner of the desk. And then in front of her reared up another cock. A big one. Sadia was proud of her skill as a fellatrice – and it was that cold a feeling, just pride; she didn't take a passionate pleasure in it – she was aware that most men were putty in the hands of a good cocksucker and in the past she had sealed many a deal with a deep throat. Here, however, her mouth was just being used as a convenient place to offload some spunk. But just at the moment she had to deal with it somehow.

She tried to close her mind down and just open her mouth. But the violence of the invasion took her by surprise and she almost choked as the massive thing plunged into her, seeking the soft caress of her throat. Sadia tried to hang onto her pride at being good at this and held the man back by pushing him away with her hands before allowing him deeper entry, but at a speed that suited her. It worked.

Behind her the secretary finished and pulled out; she assumed he had come inside her, she had been too busy at the other end to notice. She felt another cock slide into her cunt, she had no idea of whether or not she was wet or whether his ease of entry was due entirely to the amount of sperm she was leaking down there. But the entry rammed her forwards onto the cock in her mouth and was she rewarded by feeling it swell and begin to jerk. She grabbed the thick shaft to try and ease the vigour of the mouth fucking the cock's owner wanted to give her and managed to contain him. He pulled away abruptly and she was only just able to draw breath before another man was there, getting applause and laughter from his colleagues by slapping her face with his cock. She was distracted by the man behind her coming and slamming her backwards and forwards in his ecstasy. She desperately reached for the cock in front of her face and began to masturbate it. He wasn't having that however and her hand was slapped away and the head presented to her mouth.

She swallowed and took him in, although her eyes bulged as she felt another buggery commence.

Eventually it seemed to her that as she became more and more inert and supine, the more that attracted them. Sometimes they didn't bother to penetrate her, just masturbated over her as she lay sprawled across the desk. She vaguely felt spatterings on her back and in her hair as the use of her two nether entrances continued until eventually they were all finished with her. For a long time there was quiet and then she heard them leave and tried to push herself up. Her hands were sticky with sperm and slipped on the polished wood that was itself spattered with the stuff. She tried again and made it this time; shakily pushing herself upright and brushing hair out of her eyes. The office was empty apart from the president, sitting calmly beside her in his chair.

"We.......we have a deal then?"

"Indeed we do, Countess. We will keep our side of it, please ensure that you keep your side of it."

He looked at her and suddenly she saw the full ruthlessness of him. What she had just been through was nothing more than a warning shot across the bows. If she didn't have her team fully up to strength and ready to go in eight weeks, she and plenty others of her female staff could face far worse. A vision of Angel's face swam across her mind's eye and she determined that she would never see it looking as hers must just now.

Moving slowly and painfully she began to dress again and walked stiffly back to her car.

It was a blessing that Angel wasn't there to see the state of her when she got back to the stable. In fact she managed to get back to her quarters, shower and change before anyone saw her. Angel was in England for a few days with what money the stable had and Sadia still had another job to do before she returned.

She went to the office and eased her tender bottom onto her chair before reaching for the phone. From outside, down on the training ground came the sounds of a punishment beating being counted out. Smiling she listened, picturing the victim stretched out in one of the big frames; the squad all lined up to witness the punishment and the lashes being called.

She raised her eyebrows as the total passed thirty lashes and kept going. Someone had really been shirking!

At forty the punishment ceased and Sadia pictured the long lash being coiled away neatly for next time. It encouraged her. Discipline was good and the squad was well trained. She had had a tougher afternoon of it than she had expected but she had got what she wanted. Men followed their cocks – always had done; always would. And a sensible woman could ensure they went the way she wanted them to. She would win through and so would the Girl Squad.

She dialled a number and sat back, wincing just slightly.

"Eric dahhhling!" she cooed as the call was answered. "Can I drop around and see you some time this week? What? Well, it's a bit of a favour I need. No! No! Everything's fine! .....Yes! Friday will be perfect. I'll fly in Thursday night and stay at the Imperial. It'll be simply lovely to see you again, dahling! Mwah!"

She sat back and relaxed. At least she knew she had Eric wrapped around her little finger. Angel had been quite right, just a fuck every now and then to keep him happy and he would stump up the cash. For another twenty slaves she might have to consider a blow job – she rolled her tongue round her mouth, recalling the taste of sperm – but that was nothing she couldn't handle either; just so long as Angel didn't have to watch!

CHAPTER THREE

Angel gunned her hired car along another mile of boundary road. Beside her the high stone wall of The Lodge ran, topped with razor wire and backed by dense woodland. She had ignored her sat nav once she had reached the main gate, late on a fine summer afternoon, and had instead set out to try and get an impression of the size of the estate. Of course everyone with any connection to the world of SM knew of The Lodge, but even she had not realised just how big it was. For mile after mile the wall stretched with the tall trees behind it allowing not the slightest glimpse of what went on within.

It was the UK's premier SM club, and specifically for male doms. Angel of course had no problem with submissive females, she adored them as much as the next Master or Mistress, but she wasn't sure how the members would react to her. The world of The Lodge and the arenas was about as male dominated as it was possible to get – as recent events attested to vividly. But there was no help for it. The CSL stable that was contained within The Lodge's parklands, was the only quick source of fresh blood. Someone had beaten them to it but there was still talent for hire and she needed all she could get her hands on.

She came to a crossroads and took the road to her right, keeping the wall on her right and eventually came back to the massive gates. She wound her window down and sounded the intercom buzzer. A girl answered almost instantly.

"Angela Smythe for Carlo Suarez," she said curtly.

"Please use the main car park in front of the house and you'll find the check in desk in the main hall, just up the steps and through the lobby."

The gates began to swing ponderously open and Angel drove through, finding herself on a drive lined with stately lime trees. She followed it for over a mile before coming to a rise and, breaking out from under the tree covering, she found herself at The Lodge proper. The car park stretched away to her left once she driven past the imposing frontage of the house itself, and she found a space, took her bag out of the boot and looked around. The parkland swept down and out to all sides, surrounding the house's commanding position on its hill. A golf course had been laid out immediately below the slope. Over to her right she caught a glint of sunlight off water and could just make out a lake beyond some stands of trees. It could all be nothing more than a very select country house hotel, she thought as she turned to face the house. But then you saw the ponies and traps outside the front door.

Angel smiled as she took in the bridled and restrained ponies with scarlet plumes nodding above their heads and the beautifully tooled blinkers. One pony had silver cones on her nipples, the other had an ornate, steel necklace on that hung down over her chest and between her breasts. They were tethered, still harnessed between the shafts of their traps, to a rail that was mounted on the wall beside a sweeping staircase that led up to the enormous front doors.

As she approached the house, Angel could see the ponies were sweating and they stamped and shook their heads irritably as the flies bothered them. She also noted approvingly that both carried criss crossing pink stripes across their backs and buttocks from the driving whips that now stood in their rests beside the drivers' seats.

One of the front doors opened and a girl came out. Angel had of course heard of The Lodge's Housegirls but had not seen one before and she had to admit, she did look stunning. The girl was a blonde wearing a long, old fashioned, full length dress in sky blue satin. She was clearly practised in wearing it because she held the full skirt up just enough to allow her to run down the stairs. The very low cut bodice allowed Angel to see the delectable mounds of breastflesh shake and ripple as she did so.

"Hello, Madam! May I help you at all?" If the girl was startled to see a woman at The Lodge who wasn't a Housegirl, she hid it well.

"No, it's okay thanks. I'm just going to check in," Angel told her and began to climb the stairs.

The girl curtsied prettily and went to the ponies. She pushed her way between them and unhitched their reins, then clicking her tongue she backed them up a little. One of the ponies, with black hair, cavilled and tried to wrench her reins from the girl's hand. Angel was about to put her case down and go and help but saw the girl gather both ponies' reins into one hand swiftly and skilfully, then use her free hand to deliver three ringing smacks to the skittish pony's bottom.

"Settle down Amber!" she scolded and took the reins again, jerking them harshly. The pony settled at once and the girl resumed leading the pair round towards the back of the house, where Angel assumed, the stables were. She was impressed, the girl was obviously not just a pretty face.

Inside the front door, the illusion of a country house hotel took hold again and Angel looked around the lobby at the golf bags and golf shoes, the fishing rods – the day's catch laid out on the tiles floor in front of them – a hotel with a very masculine clientele, she corrected herself, and tensing in readiness for whatever reaction she might get she pushed on, opening a further door into the main hall.

Although it was still only late afternoon, the chandeliers were already lit and across the seeming acres of rich, crimson carpet, the light fell on girls dressed similarly to the one she had already seen as they hurried back and forth carrying trays of drinks to and from the lounges over on her left. To her right she glimpsed through an open door, a large dining room with tables laid with crisp, white, linen cloths. Girls, again in those curious dresses, were busily laying out cutlery and placing glasses on each table. Beyond that door and a couple more, a wide staircase swept up to meet a mirror image one from the other side of the hall at a landing. Portraits of men and women in eighteenth and nineteenth century clothes, stared down from the walls.

"Can I help you…..Miss Smythe, isn't it?"

Angrily Angel realised she'd been standing and gawping like a peasant invited up to the Big House. From behind a desk by the left hand staircase, another Housegirl was smiling over at her.

Angel went across and wordlessly signed herself in.

"Thank you," the girl said, when she had filled in her card. "Room 254, in the East Wing." She handed across a room key whose fob was a figure of a naked woman, hanging by her wrists, which were joined around the metal of the key ring. Angel couldn't help smiling at the attention to detail.

The girl rang a bell.

"I'll have your bags taken up to your room. Mr Suarez asked me to say he'll meet you at dinner, when you've had a chance to shower and change. Doctor Sands will come to your room in about an hour and will be pleased to show you around."

Another of the Housegirls, a brunette this time whose bodice could hardly contain her breasts, had appeared and picked up her bag.

"If Madam would follow me?" Again there was no hint of curiosity about a woman guest. The training and discipline was obviously very good.

They climbed the stairs and as Angel followed the girl she noticed something odd about her dress. It seemed that under the wide pleats of the full skirt that were sewn onto a deep waist band, there was one pleat that wasn't exactly a pleat – it looked as if, although the material overlapped quite widely, there was a split in the skirt, right between the buttocks.

As Angel followed the girl along corridor after corridor and up another staircase, she became more and more certain. And also she became more and more determined to try a bit of dominance and see if she was accepted as a domme.

"Stop!" she said at last. The girl did as she was told.

Angel came up behind her and took hold of the skirt, parting it where she thought it was split and sure enough, under an overlap of satin, the skirt opened. The girl's stocking clad thighs were revealed and her naked buttocks. Angel smiled when she saw them. They bore the unmistakable traces of a recent caning. And a good one as well, she judged, by the yellowing bruises.

The girl looked over her shoulder at her, a little nervously.

"That's a good caning! And the skirt opens so you can be groped or fucked, I take it?"

The girl seemed relieved, as if she was used to this – and Angel supposed she was!

"Thank you, Madam. Monsieur Poillerat does deliver a very hard caning! And yes, we can be grope......

um.....enjoyed by any of the members at any time. However, if we're found out, we get punished."

Angel gestured the girl on and followed, smiling broadly. She approved of a rule that stipulated that the submissive was at fault for her superior breaking the said rule. Very right and proper.

Her room had superb views over the lake and the woods and hills beyond – all still within the perimeter walls. It also had a four poster double bed with, and Angel checked straight away, chains hanging from each post.

She decided on a bath and was still only wrapped in her short, towelling robe and was drying her hair when there was a knock on the door. She considered asking the person to wait but then shrugged. Whoever it was, in this place they were hardly likely to be thrown by female undress.

At the door stood a neat, trim figured woman, slightly shorter than herself with cropped fair hair. She was wearing a strapless, full length evening dress in beige and although she wasn't big breasted, her nipples peaked the material very obviously. She had the sort of athletic figure that Angel liked on other women.

"Carlo asked me to drop by and help you settle in," the woman said.

Angel draped one arm over the top of the door and cocked her hip, giving the woman a slow up and down look.

"That was kind of him," she said after a few seconds.

"Whoa!" the woman said holding up a hand, palm outwards. "I'm Doctor Sands. Don't worry, there's plenty of subby playthings to go around, believe me! But I'm just here to show you round and help you understand how it all works."

Angel shrugged and grinned without embarrassment, then held out her hand as she stepped back to invite the woman in.

"I'm Angela Smythe. Most call me Angel."

"Hi, I'm Chrissie. I'm also vet to the CSL stable."

As soon as the arenas and stables entered the conversation, the ice was broken and Angel dressed while they spoke of training regimes, injuries, cures and the scandalous price of slaves just now.

When Angel had booked her room, the girl she had spoken to had warned her that dinners were formal affairs at The Lodge and so she had come prepared and slipped a little black number over just a thong. It was knee length and quite modestly high at the neckline. Neither woman had been the slightest bothered by Angel's almost complete nudity as she dressed; Chrissie only commenting, "Hmm! Nice tits!" when Angel had shrugged off the short wrap.

Now she stepped into a pair of outrageously high-heeled designer sandals and Chrissie nodded approvingly.

"Now, before we go down, let me tell you which women are available to you and which are off limits."

Angel was all ears.

"I'm afraid you can't use the Housegirls unless a member expressly gives you permission. Whether the girl is directly owned by the club or on loan from her owner while he's in residence, the members pay for them and have owner's rights. However, you can use a pony and I'll take you for a drive around the grounds tomorrow before you get down to work."

Angel was fine with that.

"With CSL it's different. You're hoping to hire some stock, so feel free to play with the slaves or the grooms as you please. No whipping outside of training for the slaves who've been booked unfortunately, they're in strict run-up now for the next games. But the grooms are gorgeous! I've got sort of ownership of one of them, and believe me they can take all the play you'll want to dish out!"

"Sounds good to me! But what's all this about the split skirts on the Housegirls? It sounds perfectly fair but I don't understand why the rule's there in the first place."

"Ah! When The Lodge was set up, Madame Stalevsky who trains and organises the Housegirls, didn't want them being fiddled with while they were doing domestic work. But John Carpenter who owns the whole thing – you'll meet him at dinner – wanted them available so he had the slit put in and to pacify Madame with the compromise, if any girl is caught being played with, she gets the beating and the member pays a small fine. That way everyone's happy."

Dinner was quite simply superb. She and Chrissie sat at John Carpenter's table with Carlo Suarez and his two assistants, Brian and Tony. Over the soup and fish – a fillet of Sea Bass, simply, yet exquisitely prepared and presented – talk of the arenas flowed easily. Carlo was a burly man, not much taller than herself, whose shoulders threatened to burst his dinner jacket.

He was a legend in Angel's world, the man who had trained Blondie – the most famous of all gladiatrices, and somehow, Angel's squad was going to have to face her at the Orange team's arena. Her two opposite numbers, Brian and Tony were polite and helpful but the Housegirls, leaning over the diners to provide or remove courses, were a constant source of distraction. Their breasts so nearly on blatant display.....but not quite.

Carlo leaned across to her at one point, when her lambs' livers with melted onion had been served and the girl's breasts had brushed her bare shoulder.

"Don't worry. In the Common Room afterwards, you can enjoy yourself. And if you want me to send a groom over later....." He grinned and left the sentence hanging.

"Thank you Carlo. I think I might need to take you up on that," she replied and lifted a glass of a light Rousillon Villages to him.

The Common Room was on the first floor and was vast. In here, any girl, even if she had been booked for bedroom service was fair game. A member who wanted to play with a girl in relative peace, could take her to one of the dungeons.

For Angel it was a mixed blessing. There were wonderful pieces of bondage furniture and racks upon racks of implements to use on the compliant flesh available. The men were unfailingly polite and invited her on several occasions to discipline this or that girl, hung in a frame or bent backwards over a bench.

Her demonstration of breast beating was warmly received; a naked blonde was shackled for her – the Housegirls' dresses were quickly shed with the use of one zip – and she was able to explain how, by taking one's time and varying the target of the beating, a sub could be kept at boiling point for a very long time, until she was tearfully begging for an orgasm. Once she had driven the blonde to that point, she surprised her audience by abandoning the whip, a sturdy flogger, and instead simply grabbing the girl's nipples and twisting, pulling and pinching them simultaneously. The resultant yell of combined agony and orgasmic release, temporarily hushed the entire room, before enthusiastic applause took over.

Smiling, she resumed her seat with Carlo, Chrissie and the rest of the party for liqueurs. The naked girlflesh was delectable but some of the men it was submitting to Angel found less than attractive. So on one hand the sight of a kneeling girl with her mouth wide open to encompass an impressive erection, was pleasant enough for her but on the other, the sight of the man to whom the erection belonged, rather deflated her arousal. She could take men like Brian, Carlo and Tony – fellow athletic dominants, but not some of the others.

When she decided to call it a day in order to have a clear head for the next day, she gratefully accepted Carlo's offer of sending across a groom called Helga.

She undressed quickly and slid under the quilt in the dark, lying quietly and just idly teasing her clitoris as she waited for the girl. At last there was a soft knock at the door and when she answered, the girl slid in.

"Mistress? I'm Helga and Carlo told me I'm yours tonight."

Angel propped herself up on one arm.

"Get your clothes off and eat my pussy!" she ordered.

There was a rustling in the dark and then Angel felt the warmth of another body slide in beside her. It was quite a turn on to realise she didn't even know what the girl looked like. She was just a body to be used for her pleasure. Her nose caught a hint of perfume and soap as the girl started to wriggle down the bed to service her.

The evening had left her on the edge of release and just a few licks on her clitoris made her come.

After that her hands explored a body which had breasts of quite adequate size with long, rather slender nipples and narrow hips. However, her cunt was extremely elastic and Angel was able to fist her after only a few minutes' penetration with her hand. She orgasmed with pretty little cries and whimpers. In the dark it came as something of a surprise for Angel to discover that the girl was branded. Her fingers traced out a rectangle on her hip within which were the letters CS and L. Helga murmured proudly and contentedly as her Mistress for the night traced the outlines and admired the brand.

Angel made her go down on her again and had her sleep between her spread legs so that she could continue first thing in the morning.

She slept deeply and woke to see the sun already shining through the heavy curtains. Between her spread thighs was a delightful tickling sensation from where Helga's hair lay on her thighs. She gave the girl a gentle kick and sighed as, without any demur, she got down to licking her cunt out all over again.

When she had dismissed the girl, Angel showered, dressed in her jeans and shirt and went down to breakfast.

She felt slightly more at home after the previous night and when the waitress brought her croissants to her table she availed herself of the split in the back of her dress and felt her way into a very moist cunt. The buttocks were markedly ridged she noted as she withdrew her fingers and wiped them on her bottom.

"You in the dungeons last night?" she asked.

"Yes, Madam," the girl replied. Angel looked at her more closely and noted the dark rings beneath the eyes. The girl smiled at her and left.

The same girl served her coffee and Angel repeated her explorations, this time taking time to stimulate the clitoris as well as the vagina. The girl's hips began to rock in response and Angel looked around to see if anyone was going to notice and stop her, but there was no one and she kept the frigging up until a long groan escaped the girl and Angel let her go.

She was licking her fingers and savouring the mixture of tastes with the coffee when Chrissie arrived.

They shared a sociable meal while around them the men ate, planned their day and some reserved girls for playing with later by attaching disks with their room number on them to their collars.

"I thought we'd go for a drive while they're getting the slaves mucked out, washed and fed over at CSL," Chrissie said, then added with a smile, "besides you can't get too much of driving a good pony!"

Angel couldn't have agreed more and the two women strolled out via the front door and around to the side of the house and the stableyard. Two perfectly presented rigs awaited them and Angel saw a pretty, Asian girl brushing out one of the ponies' hair. She was dressed in a short kilt with a blouse knotted up underneath her breasts, it was the same uniform that she had seen Helga dress in hurriedly when she had been dismissed earlier that morning. Attractive, and it presented very little difficulty for someone wanting to investigate beneath the clothes.

The girl looked over at them and smiled widely, then stood back respectfully as they came closer. Beside Angel, Chrissie suddenly seemed to pull herself together and become much more positive and assertive. She strode forwards and began to inspect the ponies.

Angel noted the pretty Indian groom looking nervous and began to see what was going on. She smiled as she watched Chrissie testing the tightness of the cruppers and the correct alignment of the girths, adorned with The Lodge's crest in chromium on the front, where it widened to cover the stomach. She pulled on the bits to make sure they had been pushed securely to the backs of their mouths before the bridles had been buckled on. She looked at their backs to check on the girth buckles and found that she could slip her fingers between one pony's skin and the leather of the girth.

She turned to Angel triumphantly.

"Daft little tart always gets one detail wrong! Raika! Come here you useless slut!"

The Indian girl darted forward, her huge, expressive eyes clouded with concern.

"You've embarrassed me in front of my friend here with your sloppiness. Go and get a crop so I can thrash you!"

Dropping the slight curtsy that the short kilt would allow, the girl scuttled away.

"That the one you sort of own?" Angel asked.

"Yes. Long story. But what a lovely piece of arse!"

Angel had to agree when the girl returned and was immediately bent over a hitching rail; her arms extended on each side along the bar. Chrissie stepped forwards and lifted the short skirt, tucking it in to its own waist band to keep it out of the way. The coffee coloured buttocks were smooth and deliciously round and pert, with no sign of a crease at the tops of the silky thighs. And when she shuffled her legs apart, Angel felt a tide of hot moisture at her groin as she saw the dusky little purse of the neatly lipped cunt.

Chrissie wasted no time and cracked in a telling lash almost as soon as the groom had gone down. It was plainly a common occurrence in the yard because no one batted an eyelid at the sharp report of leather on skin.

Angel was impressed, Chrissie hadn't flicked; the groom had taken a full swing and the doctor had followed through fully as well, flattening the buttocks and sending a delicious shock wave through the flesh, even of the upper thighs. The groom gave no more than a hiss through gritted teeth and took two more with no more reaction.

Chrissie offered Angel the crop as the girl made no move to rise.

"Feel free," she said and Angel willingly stepped up to the mark behind the exquisite arse. She smiled.

The girl's submissiveness was obvious – and her Mistress had known exactly how to trigger it, by offering her up for punishment on a whim. Angel had no compunction in taking full advantage of the offer and thoroughly enjoyed adding another three crisp, buttock-rippling strokes to Raika's tally.

It was the perfect warm up for their whip arms.

As they climbed in and settled themselves, Chrissie explained that the ponies were from the stock of Housegirls, all of whom served from time to time in harness.

"But don't conclude they're all docile because of it. Some of them like to express a rebellious side between the shafts."

Angel smiled and examined the back of the pony she was now seated behind. The shoulders were broad and the back was shapely. The hips wide and the legs quite long. She wouldn't have minded betting that this beast would give a good ride anywhere –and once again she felt a tide of warm moisture at her belly.

In front of her the pony stamped her sandal-shod foot and as Angel gathered up the reins she ducked and twisted her head, pulling impatiently.

"Ah! Did Carlo tell you to give me the liveliest one in the stable?" she called across to Chrissie, smiling broadly.

"Now that'd be telling!" the doctor called back cheerfully and with a quick flick of her whip, tongue-clicked her pony up.

Angel tugged hard on the reins and brought the pony's head up before lashing it back and forehand across the buttocks.

The pony started off but was plainly skittish, shaking her head and prancing as she headed across the cobbles to follow Chrissie through an archway and out into the park. She dragged one wheel of the trap against a corner as they entered the arch and jolted the rig quite harshly. Angel whipped her again and the pony skittered sideways, her sandals' scraping and clopping echoing loudly against the stone walls of the short tunnel. Angel pursed her lips as she dragged the pony's head to face the direction of the road again and waited till they were out in the fresh air. Then she reined in with brutal force and swung the driving whip back and forth across the buttocks while holding her reins tightly.

The pony squealed through her bit and tossed her head as Angel smacked the whip cord home against her back and shoulders; she didn't stop until the pony was fully cowed and subdued and Angel was panting from the exertion of thrashing her.

Chrissie had stopped and had turned to watch over her shoulder, smiling broadly as Angel gathered herself, swept a stray lock of hair off her forehead and tongue-clicked the penitent pony forwards once more.

"Actually Carlo's instructions," she told Angel as she brought her rig alongside at a leisurely walk, "were to make sure you got an enjoyable mount!"

Angel laughed and looked at her pony's lividly striped buttocks rippling as she walked.

"I'll thank him myself," she said and flicked the pony up to a trot.

The day was fine and the two women spent a relaxing hour trotting along tracks that criss crossed the golf course before the golfers had really got started and they met Brian coming the other way at the fourteenth. In contrast to themselves he had his pony at full stretch, the rig's wheels rumbled on the dry ground and the driving whip smacked and curled high in the air above the sweat-streaked slave's back.

When he saw them he reined in so harshly the pony's feet nearly went from under her as she leaned back against the weight, tossing her head and spraying lather and sweat. At the last moment, he yanked her head round to the right and the rig did a little skid as it came to a halt.

Angel was impressed by the driving skill and by the toughness of the pony but recognised male antler rattling when she saw it and kept her face neutral.

"Good morning!" Brian called out as his pony champed at her bit and stamped in irritation at having her run interrupted.

"Which one's this?" Angel asked, unable to identify the pony from behind the heavy blinkers and bridle, although she had studied the CSL brochure online.

"This is Legs," Brian told her, stroking her back with the tip of the driving whip and making her shudder with what Angel recognised as the mingled fear and lust a slave should feel towards her owner. "She's coming on well. Just needs a bit of toughening up."

"Don't flay her too much, I might need her if she's not been booked!" Angel reminded him.

"Nah!" Brian grinned. "She'll be fine! See you at the yard."

He hauled the pony backwards a few prancing steps and then whipped her away, lashing her on with undiminished fervour.

Chrissie and Angel watched him go, admiring the speed and smoothness of the pony's gait, despite pulling a heavy, male driver.

As Brian's whip continued to play as it faded into the distance, Angel gave her own shiver of suppressed lust. There was so much deliciously submissive girlflesh on view and so little was available to her. It was not normal for her.

"Don't worry, we'll get you something a bit special to play with before the day's out!" Chrissie called as they resumed their rather more stately pace.

CHAPTER FOUR

Sadia stepped into the air conditioned, leather scented luxury of the car sent for her and sat back as it pulled away.

"Join me for dinner with some friends and we can discuss your stable's needs," Eric had said. She had outlined the problem to him on the phone once she had checked into the hotel and he had seemed oddly unsurprised and quite affable. Normally he winced audibly at the mention of any more outlay at all.

But she expected she would be able to handle him alright. She always had up till now and she smiled as she glanced down and smoothed the crisp linen of her skirt across her thighs, just a few, but tactically so important, inches above her knees. Her legs were long and shapely in any case but she had pampered them deliberately over the previous few days.

It had taken her a day or two to recover from the president's office but now she felt she was ready for whatever Eric could do to her vagina. The dear man was so eager! He practically salivated if she so much as crossed her legs. But it was so much fun watching him make a slave suffer while she and Angel made love – his infatuation had its advantages! She stretched with pleasure as she recalled the way Angel's cunt gushed with fragrant juices while Eric made a slave squeal and cry out. But on the few occasions she had allowed him to fuck her, he hadn't been too bad. So really, as long as Angel didn't have to watch, she didn't think the evening would throw up anything untoward.

And she was still convinced of that when the car swung off the road, rumbled across a wooden drawbridge, dived briefly into darkness under a barbican and finally pulled up in the main courtyard of a restored but obviously very old castle.

Eric stood back from the window as Sadia stepped out from the car and smoothed her jacket and skirt. He had waited so long for this!

He turned to his dinner guests, a group of men and women whose clothing and manner marked them out as all being of a similar rank to Sadia.

"We have the evening's main event!" he said. "After dinner I shall drive the deal through and we will add the Countess de Groncourt to the diversions that await us in the dungeons!"

A man came forwards and shook his hand. "We know how long you've planned and waited for this. It will be a pleasing entertainment indeed."

Eric laughed aloud in relief and delight.

"It had to happen! If I just kept her short of stock for long enough, she'd come crawling."

Everyone raised their glasses and drank just before a butler in full 18th century regalia ushered her into the room, which was panelled in oak and glowing in the lights.

Smiling, Eric advanced and kissed her cheek, inhaling the fragrance of her perfume and revelling in the feel of her soft skin against his.

Then, keeping his arm about her waist, he introduced her to his other guests. Sadia caught the drift of the names and titles as he smoothly guided her from group to group; they were all very rich. Perhaps these were the 'angels' who would back her purchase of new livestock.

At last, having smiled politely, shaken hands and air-kissed her way around the room, she was led to a table covered with bottles of Krug and Eric poured her a welcome glass.

"Who are all these people?" she asked. Her meetings with Eric had previously been more in offices than castles. "Can they help me?"

"No, my dear," Eric said with a strange, cold smile that Sadia didn't like the look of one bit. "They are merely the audience. Although they are fellow members of our little club, the rest of whom are held in the dungeons downstairs. But we'll see them in due course. Now let us eat and discuss our business afterwards."

Sadia was disturbed. Eric had suddenly become harsher and more stern, and she wasn't entirely sure she knew this new Eric. But the meal was superb and the talk was all about her favourite topic; slaves.

It transpired that Eric and his friends had a small and exclusive sm club all of their own and it regularly met at this location. Between full meetings there was a complement of live-in slaves tended to by managers and the various couples could come and stay and play as often as they cared to.

"But, alas!" Eric said as the meal finished and the butlers cleared away the crockery. "Business now calls. You go on without us and we'll join you soon enough."

With a scraping of chairs and excited talk of the delights waiting in the cellars below, the other guests disappeared and left Eric and Sadia alone.

"You sly old fox!" Sadia said. "All this time and you never let on about any of this!"

"I am indeed a great deal more subtle than you have given me credit for, Sadia," he told her gravely, topping up her wine glass. "Now tell me again what the problem is and let's see if I can solve it."

"It's simple. We rushed into our first games to replenish the coffers. We won and now some of the other stables are ganging up on us, using CSL stock. We're short handed and if we don't get at least twenty more good quality bitches – we're finished. Or that's what Angel thinks and I've no reason to doubt her. We've got to have the new stock before our first home games."

Eric pursed his lips and wandered slowly over to the window above the courtyard.

"Good quality stock is costing very dear just now," he said at last.

Sadia felt on safer ground here, this was more the usual Eric.

"Darling Eric. You'll find me more grateful than ever before." She went to stand behind him and put her arms round him, resting her head on his back, pressing her breasts against him.

"Hmm. You will have to be, Sadia. Indeed you will. You shall have enough for your twenty but hear my price."

He turned and looked down at her, his eyes dark and dangerous suddenly. Sadia backed away.

"In return for funding this new purchase, I will have you as my consort here whenever the club meets. And like all the other women you have just dined with, you will wear tokens of your subservience to me."

"What tokens?" Sadia asked.

"Rings," he said succinctly. "At nipples and labia."

Sadia smiled – it was all a joke! No one in their right minds would think of putting rings on her! Not the Countess de Groncourt!

"And," he continued steadily, advancing towards her, "a tag, so whoever fucks you knows who you belong to."

She struck out and landed a stinging blow on his cheek.

He merely smiled and grasped her wrist, crushing it to the point where she sank to her knees, whimpering.

"Of course, you can always refuse and the Girl Squad will die."

A vision of her darling Angel watching her stable go down to humiliating defeat after defeat, flitted in front of her mind's eye.

"Well?" he demanded, his grip tightening.

"You would make me a whore!" she spat.

"No. I would make you *my* whore!" His tone and face were calm and implacable, and Sadia knew she was doomed.

There was nothing she could do. But she had seen innumerable piercings and didn't think she could suffer them herself. It was what happened to submissive bitches, not dominants like herself. But for Angel and for the honour of her stable.........there just didn't seem to be a choice.

Eric seeming to sense her acceptance of the inevitable, relaxed his grip and allowed her to stand.

To her immense relief she was allowed an anaesthetic spray before the procedures, which were carried out in a room in the castle basements, with the other club members watching.

Eric led her down a grand flight of stairs to the main hall and from there through what must have been the original kitchens but which were now deserted and echoing. He took her through an arched door and then they descended again, this time on bare stone, spiral stairs until they emerged into surprisingly tall cellars, the roof supported by huge, thick stone pillars. Red shaded lamps provided a suitably subdued illumination. Around the door they entered by were gathered tables and sofas and on these the members she had already met reclined. Some of the women's breasts were revealed and Sadia noted that they all sported the rings she had been promised. However, what caught her attention most were the waiters – the slave managers, Eric told her – they were well-built men and naked apart from leather trousers that left their sexes naked. Most of the cocks were limp or only semi tumescent but some were thickly erect and were being energetically sucked by some of the women, who were sitting forward or leaning over the sofas' arms to service the men.

The drinks tables were glass panels resting on the backs of naked female slaves, on all fours. The slaves were held in place by slender chains running from nipple rings to rings in the stone floor and from labial rings to the same rings in the floor.

"The Countess has agreed to be my consort and will accept her marks," Eric announced and immediately there was applause, and as Eric led her on, the company stood and followed them. They went into a white-painted room with a medical bench, bright lights and cupboards and shelves of implements. A large, hooded man, again naked apart from open crotch trousers, stood beside the bench, his thickly muscled, tattooed arms crossed in front of his chest.

"Undress and then suck his cock," Eric told her bluntly. "It's for your own good. He works better when he's relaxed."

Sadia did as she was told and was rewarded by admiring comments on her legs, bottom and breasts from the assembled guests as she stripped. The man beside the bench also betrayed some arousal and by the time she knelt before him, his cock was throbbing and stirring. She leaned forwards a little and placed her hands on his hips.

"No!" Eric immediately barked. "Hands behind your back!"

She complied and felt his hands descend on her head. So it was to be a fellation where she would be mouth fucked with no control whatever. At least he tasted clean, she thought as she licked his helm and then his shaft before opening her mouth wide and gently lowering it over the huge, glistening helm, her tongue running along the meatus as she did so. He filled her mouth completely and she had no choice but to

flatten her tongue and allow him full access. Unlike the last men to have sampled her mouth, this man at least appeared to appreciate a skilful fellatrice and although his thrusts were deep, he was content to withdraw enough to allow her to tongue him on several occasions before he finally clamped her head between his large hands and fucked her mouth until she felt the splashes of thick sperm jet out into her throat and she had to swallow quickly to keep up with him. He lingered at her lips for a few moments to allow her to clean him properly and then he courteously helped her onto the bench, lifted and spread her legs into stirrups and tied her wrists to a spreader bar above her head. Sadia just had a last chance to look down at her unadorned nipples as they were sprayed and then she shut her eyes tightly once she saw the hooded man pick up the piercing needle with the gutter at its tip into which the ring would be threaded and pulled back through once the initial hole had been bored.

"We don't use a punch, Sadia," Eric explained. "We like the women to savour the experience of being decorated for us."

Scarcely half an hour later that Sadia was helped shakily to her feet and applauded as she examined herself in a mirror. The nipple rings stung bitterly but looked quite attractive she thought, but at her crotch the two rings – one in each labium – felt leaden and heavy; especially the one on her right. From that ring depended a silver tag over an inch long with the club's name on one side and Eric's name on the other. The rings were spring loaded and one end had been slotted hard into the other, she had even felt the jerk as the catches had taken. They would have to be sawn off if she wanted them removed, Eric told her gleefully.

In truth, Sadia was a little bit proud of the decorations and even spread her legs apart to see the tag dangling between her thighs. At least Angel would know how high a price she had paid for the new stock. But worries about how her lover would respond to her cunt being identified as belonging to a man and how much pain there would be when the spray wore off were put to the back of her mind as one of the men clapped his hands and instructed the managers to produce the slaves so that the evening's entertainment could continue.

CHAPTER FIVE

Angel immediately appreciated the tidy and clean appearance of the CSL stable once they had returned their ponies to The Lodge's stable and Chrissie had shown her the way to where the real business of the day would take place.

One of the grooms was hosing down the shower area, another was scrubbing the toilets and a third was leading out two slaves on tongue rings and leashes who were required for training in the covered arena that Chrissie had shown her on their way round.

Depressingly however, eight of the stalls had red disks hung above their doors to signify that the slave had been hired.

Carlo himself was there to greet her once she had had time to take a brief glance around. He was accompanied by a striking woman who wore black suede thigh boots with her groom's uniform and who was collared and – Angel couldn't help noticing – branded in exactly the same place as Helga. She had a thick head of copper coloured hair.

"This is Patti Coldwell," Carlo told her. "She's head groom."

Immediately Angel could feel the tension in the air between the head groom and the doctor beside her, but felt it wise to ignore it for the moment and smiled and shook the newcomer's hand.

But Carlo was eager to show off his stock, even those ones who had been booked and for the next hour or two, Angel was kept busy.

Inevitably the first stall he went to was Blondie's and Angel was thrilled to be able to pat and fondle the greatest fighting slave the arenas had produced while Carlo fed her some titbits. She was nearly as tall as Angel was and a little more heavily built. Like all the slaves her wrists were clipped neatly behind her back and one ankle was chained to the rear wall of the stall. It was similar to the discipline that Angel herself imposed on her senior fighters. The squad were too numerous to marshal so carefully and were only chained at nights. But as Carlo fussed over her and boasted of her achievements, Angel was able to appreciate Blondie's superb physique. The breasts were high and large, with no sign of any sag about them and the nipples had stood to attention the minute her master had summoned her. Angel caressed them and was impressed that they bore no trace of any of the piercings they would have been subjected to over her years of enslavement. Indeed, as Angel ran her hands over the slave's body she was amazed at how silky smooth the skin was despite the punishment it so regularly took in the arenas. She slid her hand down to the groin and as Carlo fed her a piece of her favourite shortbread, she spread her legs obediently allowing Angel's hand to encounter a large and hard clitoris just in front of a warm and moist vagina that offered no resistance to Angel's fingers.

She commented on the fact to Carlo, who pointed to the disk above the stall.

"She knows she's going into a games soon, and there'll be plenty of time for her to be played with in the evenings," he replied and ruffled her hair affectionately, then grasped her left breast hard, making her jerk her head up in surprise and clatter her tongue ring against her teeth as her eyes closed in pleasure at the harsh caress.

"Mine are the same," Angel said. "But I'm surprised she still gets so turned on, after all she's seen and done pretty well everything there is to see and do in an arena."

Carlo shrugged. "It's what she's for. And even after all this time she loves to know I'm pleased with her."

Angel took another look at the famous slave and noticed this time that around the eyes closed in pleasure were fine networks of faint lines.

"Have you started cutting down on the number of times you hire her out?" she asked. Carlo looked at her sharply.

"Sorry, it was just something I heard on the grapevine."

Carlo nodded, slapped Blondie hard on the buttocks and moved on.

"It's something I'm aware of," he said quietly.

In the next stall was Ayesha, who made no attempt to approach them until Carlo produced a piece of cake. But Angel couldn't help noticing that whereas Blondie's face had lit up at the sight of Carlo, Ayesha remained aloof. The tour went on and she met the two big blondes, Ox and Trouble who would form the nucleus of any whip melee. Beside them, as she would be in the arena was the menacing form of Fiji, the tall Polynesian who, like Ayesha, held herself aloof but allowed herself to be fondled and felt. Again she was exhibiting all the signs of a slave eager to experience pain for others' pleasure. Angel wiped her fingers on the girl's stomach and admired the gleam on the dark skin.

Eventually they reached the stalls of the slaves not hired in for the upcoming games and Angel started to really concentrate.

It was hardly a state secret that the ones the Orange team had booked were especially effective at the strength and endurance events. Apart from whip fighting, Ox and Trouble were extremely good at paired log pulling. Blondie, Jet and Ayesha were almost without equal when it came to pursuit running – where a naked slave was given a head start by a mounted man and then hunted down. The object for the slave was to make as many laps of the arena as possible before she was brought down by his whip. Fiji was as tough as teak at boxing.

The first of the available slaves was Purdy, she was a big breasted girl of part Canadian, part Italian descent according to her provenance from auction. Once Brian had tamed her she had turned out to be a very useful runner in both single pony races and in the six slave chariot races – despite the handicap of her large breasts. She came to the front of her stall immediately and nuzzled Angel's hand to see if she had any treats.

"She can hold her own in pursuit running," Carlo told her as she fed a liqueur chocolate to the slave. "If the Orange team use the rest of our stock in earlier events and not in the later ones like the running, this one could give you an edge there."

Angel made a mental note and they moved on to a redhead called Sam. She was wiry and not as sturdy as some of her more famous peers but when Angel bent to feel the sinews of her calves and thighs, she found them surprisingly well developed. It came as something of a bonus to find that her juices were flowing thickly and fragrantly as well, when Angel allowed herself the luxury of feeling yet another cunt.

"She's not well known yet, but I reckon she's worth a good few points in the pens and in whip melees. I've seen her give Ox and Jet a few problems in boxing and wrestling as well," Carlo told her as she patted the slave's flank and let her go back into her stall.

"That's the one thing that bothers me," she replied. "Will they really pull out all the stops if they're up against their own stable?"

Carlo favoured her with a broad grin. "Come with me. I'll show you," he told her and led her towards the door out to the yard. However, on their way, from the room at the far end of the stables came the unmistakable sound of a whip being plied in a fast and steady rhythm. To Angel it could only mean a punishment beating, a more leisurely pace usually marked out a beating given for pleasure. She cocked an eyebrow at Carlo.

"I thought whipping was off the menu until after the games," she said.

"It is – except for Beast. If she doesn't get it regularly every few days, she's a nightmare. You want to see?"

"My bitches are going to be up against her, so, yeah. I'd like a look."

The room turned out to be a fully equipped dungeon cum playroom and the woman who had been introduced to Angel as Patti was hard at work.

Before her was a naked slave, stretched out, face down on an X cross that had been pivoted in its frame to lie parallel to the floor.

Angel's attention was also drawn immediately to the fact that Patti had stripped off her knotted blouse and was working in only her skirt and boots. Her magnificent, pale breasts swung and joggled deliciously as she wielded the lash, which was a heavy strap about a foot long that came to a point.

It was also clear that she was working hard and was biting her bottom lip in concentration as she punished the body below her. When she saw Carlo she stepped back straight away and adopted a submissive stance with her hands behind her back.

Carlo went to the slave's head and pulled it up so that Angel could see the tousled hair framing a not unattractive, gamine sort of face that wore a feral grin. The girl poked her heavily ringed tongue out at Carlo. Angel knew this was commonly a gesture of submission on the part of tongue-ringed slaves but here it seemed a deliberate invitation to Carlo to do his worst.

"Don't tell anyone I said this." Carlo turned towards Angel, still holding Beast by her hair. "But don't put any slave you've paid a lot for in against this one. She don't know when she's beaten, she's a real head case maso bitch. At boxing only Blondie and Ayesha can take her. At wrestling Jet, Tigre and Blondie can handle her. But she's crap at any running event and she reckons log pulling is heaven on earth and just laps up the whip instead of working. So they'll use her for the rough stuff. My advice is to let 'em and in the pens give her one of yours that you can afford to lose to play with, you can only lose one set of points."

"Thanks Carlo, I'll bear that in mind," Angel said as they turned to go.

Patti stepped forward once more and resumed the beating with all the gusto she had previously shown and as Angel turned to look back just as she was leaving, it was to see her slamming the whip down the buttock crease and along the crack of the French slave's cunt, which was provoking nothing more than an enthusiastic bucking of the hips. Angel stored away Carlo's advice as they made their way towards the arena.

Brian was watching Lucky and Blackie sparring as they entered. It was a gentle workout in a wrestling ring but as soon as Carlo entered he called out and brought things to a halt.

"Angel wants to see how hard these bitches will go against each other if they meet in an arena!"

"Good question," Brian agreed cheerfully. "Want to see them box?"

Angel nodded. With the full studded tack on it was impossible for one slave not to hurt her opponent.

A few minutes later she was standing with one foot on the bottom rope and leaning on a corner post as the two slaves ducked back into the ring, looking very different to the naked wrestlers who had left it. They both wore leather corsets and Angel could see the little tines denting the soft breast flesh along the line of the cups and she knew perfectly well that the studs lined the whole of the fronts of the corsets. They also wore leather thongs and these were studded as well. An uppercut in one of these contests was usually a stopping blow – if only because one contestant was helplessly orgasming.

Each girl had straps wound around her knuckles and inside these were weights.

These made the action slow and deliberate as the heavy fists were swung and gave the girls more time to take evasive action. It also meant that the crowds could follow the action better from the terraces as the movements were exaggeratedly slow.

Angel was impressed from the moment Carlo waved the girls together and stepped out of the ring. The contestants went at each other with all the venom she could want, trying to get knees into groins and fists swinging at breasts. And when the blows did connect, it was quite clear that they weren't being pulled. Blackie's long, coal black hair swung and swirled as she danced and ducked, while Lucky's slender arms nevertheless swung heavy and telling blows when she was fortunate enough to connect. The arena began to echo to the grunts of effort and pain, heavy thuds became more frequent as the girls began to tire. In the arenas, this was what the crowds would be waiting for; the moment the slaves came together and began to slug it out until one went down.

Angel, however, had seen all she needed. There was no point in risking damage to stock she would need to hire in. She signalled to Carlo and he stepped back into the ring. Immediately the two girls parted and partially bent forwards, bracing their hands on their thighs, their mouths open and their chests heaving for breath. The two trainers petted them and told them they had been good, giving them playful smacks to buttocks and flanks as they began to unlace the corsets. Angel was impressed. She recognised the well-trained slave's eagerness to please her owner, no matter what.

Her thoughts were interrupted however by her mobile vibrating in her jeans pocket. It was Sadia, and the prospect of talking with her lover caused the warmth between her legs, started by watching shapely slaves fight each other, to increase to a hot liquid feeling deep in her belly.

"Hello, darling," Sadia's voice caressed her ear. "How are things going at your end?"

Angel had walked a few yards away when she answered the call and now she turned to look back and saw both slaves naked, arms raised above their heads as the men examined them, running their hands over the quivering breasts, testing the dents where the tines had dug in.

"Pretty well," she replied. "I think there's more talent here than those bastards realised, so we might still be able to give them a couple of nasty surprises. How's things with you?"

"Fine." Angel was immediately aware of the slight hesitation in Sadia's reply but held her tongue. "We'll get the twenty extra we need. No problem."

"But," Angel supplied after a second's silence. "There's got to be a 'but'."

"Let's just say the price was unexpectedly high. D'you know, Eric belongs to this wonderful club and they put on a show you would have loved. Some of the best bullwhipping I've seen in ages! And while some fabulous wine was served too! I think we watched eight girls in all being worked on. The needles were gorgeous, darling. One girl got thirty in her tits alone. Honestly I came almost as much as the slut did! And the sex afterwards was to die for………."

Angel let Sadia rattle on for a few moments until she came to a stop.

"You haven't told me what price we're paying," she said eventually.

"The money's about what I expected but there is something else………I've got a few things to show you……..I had to agree to wear some things for Eric."

"What things?"

Angel felt her stomach ache with anger as she listened to Sadia's reply. In her mind she saw her Mistress and lover's perfect body defiled by men. Her lovely nipples which she so often had licked and nipped at to draw sighs of pleasure from her, rubbery and quivering under her tongue, were now pierced so cruelly by hard steel. What was right and proper on a slave – a submissive – was an outrage on Angel's beloved Countess.

And as for her beautiful cunt, nestling between her long and silky-smooth thighs. The soft, plump lips were now brutally holed and even a tag proclaiming it the property of a man hung from it. Angel could almost taste the acrid, horrible metal as she imagined lying between Sadia's legs, tonguing her as she had so loved to do while they listened to the music of a slave being played with beside them.

She grimaced as she imagined having to lift the evidence of a man's presumptuous arrogance out of her way before she could forage in her ladyship's fragrant honeypot.

From the ring came the voices of Brian and Carlo as Tony came to take the two slaves back to the stable.

Angel turned back, almost shaking with rage.

"Okay if we send 'em back?" Brian asked as she walked across to the ring, trying to calm her anger. "Or do you want to play with one of them? I know watching them go at each other sometimes leaves me in need of a shag or a beating."

Angel stopped at the ropes as an idea occurred to her.

"No, let them go. It's ok. But I wouldn't mind a bit of release, how about you and I go a few rounds?"

Tony paused in the act of clipping Lucky's leash to her tongue ring and cocked an eyebrow at Brian. Carlo just gave one of his grins and leaned on the ropes opposite Angel. Brian himself looked thoroughly startled at first and then relaxed and treated Angel to a slow look of such blatant lust that it re-ignited her determination to be revenged on the whole male gender for what had been done to Sadia.

At a nod from Carlo, Tony led the slaves away and Angel ducked into the ring.

"Wrestling and kick-boxing; anything goes, no holds barred except gouging or scratching. Stripped to pants," she said. It was the sort of bout the slaves were used to in training and in the pens and the arenas themselves.

Brian shrugged amiably and stripped off his shirt. Angel did likewise and unhitched her bra. If she hadn't been seething with anger, she might have been pleased with the looks her breasts fetched as they swung freely on her chest. With no ceremony she kicked off her shoes and unzipped her jeans, tugged them down her legs and pulled them off, then straightened up in just her thong.

She saw that Brian now faced her in just a tight pair of boxers, again had she been more in a mood to appreciate the view she might have been impressed with his physique. But as it was she allowed herself the luxury of letting her temper take over and she plunged joyfully into the physical release of combat.

She rushed him and ducked at the last moment, grabbing his legs and pulling while she used her shoulder into his midriff. Taken by surprise he toppled backwards but immediately managed to get his arms round her chest and squeeze as she followed him down onto the earth floor of the ring. His hard muscled forearms squeezed her breasts but she registered only the imprisonment and not the sharp sensations from her nipples. She jabbed downwards hard with her elbow and broke the hold, springing away back onto her feet and delivering a drop kick as he came surging up after her. He took a step backwards. She swung a punch at his face and he swayed out of its way easily then caught her with a roundhouse kick that jarred the whole of her left side as his foot crashed into her ribs. She staggered for a moment but was able to swing a right hook into his ribs before he could fully steady himself. He didn't flinch and simply grabbed her wrist to swing her round and send her crashing backwards into a corner post. She tottered forwards, partly winded but saw him coming and as he reached for her she jabbed hard with her right and caught him on the chin. He staggered back, hurt for the first time and she tried to repeat the blow but he fended her off and countered with two rapid jabs to her ribs that stopped her in her tracks.

For a few seconds they circled each other warily, Brian tried to tempt her into a finger lock but Angel knew she couldn't win a straight contest of strength and ignored it. As she moved, she could feel the weight of her breasts shift on her chest and Brian's eyes kept flicking down towards them. She waited till it happened again and delivered a roundhouse kick that hurt him again as her foot slammed into his cheek. She tried to spin round fast enough to deliver another but found that he was ready and had caught her foot before it could connect. With both hands he twisted it and she screamed as she had to pirouette and collapse onto her face to avoid the pain. He was onto her at once, slamming down onto her back and crushing her. He dropped her foot and grabbed her right arm instead, twisting it high up her back. She knew his grip was too strong for her to break but at least she had got some hard blows in and he would remember her for a few days. The exertion had also allowed her to release her anger and she felt calmer and able to concentrate on her job once more. She would have to see what could be done for poor Sadia in due course.

But for now........she bowed to the inevitable and fell forward, letting her body relax in submission.

Brian recognised the sign and climbed off her, coming to stand over her, breathing hard.

"Good fight, Angel. Thanks."

He reached down to help her up and she struck.

She grabbed his wrist and twisted it savagely. At the same time she swung around on the ground and raised her legs as he fell. She got one foot under the arm she was twisting and the other up beside his jaw. Then she stretched her legs and pulled as he hit the ground, twisting his wrist upwards and holding him with rigid legs.

"Submit!" she hissed as she exerted her full strength and heard him cry out as his hand was bent up over his forearm. She adjusted her grip and was able to start bending in his little finger on itself. He cried out again, recognising that she could break it. She pushed hard at his wrist again and he answered her demand to submit.

Panting, she released him and immediately scrabbled away out of his reach before standing up.

Brian got slowly to his feet nursing his injured arm.

"You sly bitch!" he said, though to her irritation he was still smiling.

She tossed her hair back and reached for her jeans. "Anything goes, right? Anything at all in an arena."

"She's got a point," Carlo put in.

"Yeah. Ha! That'll teach me not to be a gentleman!" Brian even managed a short laugh as he worked his sore shoulder.

Angel couldn't help feeling cheated at how easily he accepted her sharp practice as a sort of good joke at his expense and didn't seem at all humbled or shamed.

At dinner that evening he even recounted the incident and Angel felt that she was being patronised in some strange way. If it had been her, she would have been enraged by being tricked and shown up in front of companions! He couldn't possibly be a proper dom if he could take such things in his stride, she decided.

But it was odd how much she felt the need for a sub that night and asked Chrissie if she could have a groom, a bit earlier than on the previous night if possible as she needed to play.

"Have Patti," the vet said. "I'll have her sent to Dungeon Five if you like. It's got some good frames and a medical bench."

That sounded like what she needed and Chrissie summoned a Housegirl to take a message over to the CSL stable.

After dinner she excused herself from liqueurs in the Common Room and followed Chrissie's directions downstairs from the back of the main hall and along well lit corridors, down further steps until finally she arrived at a low ceilinged, stone walled passage with thick wooden doors along one side with grilles set in each. She pushed open the one with the number 5 on it and went in.

There were two slaves inside. One was being worked on by a Lodge member over on Angel's left. Standing with her back to the wall and to which she was chained, she was having her breasts bound. They were delightfully marked from the crop that was lying on a whipping bench just behind the member and Angel could see from the paddle, whip and packets of sterile needles that they were about to get more punishment. Both looked up briefly as she entered, smiled and then returned their attention to the breast binding, the girl's eyes were wide and excited.

Patti stood opposite the door, fully dressed but with her hands clipped together behind her back and a leash running from the O ring on her collar to a hook on the wall.

Angel went straight to her and unknotted the woman's blouse, freeing the large, pale breasts and began to massage them.

The day's events; Sadia's decorations and the fight with Brian and his subsequent calm acceptance of the result, had left her confused. But here at least she knew what she was and what was going to happen. Her hands felt the woman's nipples harden under them, she watched her eyes close in pleasure and her breathing deepen, then she leaned closer and let her cheek brush Patti's.

"I'm going to thrash them so hard!" she whispered. "And then I'll whip your back and your arse before I let you lick me out."

Patti groaned in appreciation of the cruelties to come and Angel fumbled under the short skirt to find soft and engorged labia with a sticky flood of fragrant juices between them. The clitoris stood out hard and urgent. Angel rasped it mercilessly and fetched further groans from Patti. Then she stood back, slipped off the dress she had worn for dinner and took Patti's lead.

She decided on a padded bench to start with and once Patti was naked had her lie face up along its length before fastening her ankles and wrists to the bottoms of the legs.

She selected a flogger with square-cut, leather tails and stood over the stretched body, stroking and teasing the quivering breasts and the moist lips between the spread thighs. Then she struck, a quick flick at the breasts followed by a heavier strike between the legs. Then a heavy strike across the nipples, another across the stomach and a flick to the cunt. Patti's head snapped up at the heavier lashes, her lips pursed at the stinging. Angel continued the treatment never letting her guess where the next strike would fall, knowing that would intensify the experience for the full-breasted slave. She watched in pleasure as the stomach began to flutter and the hips began to undulate as she continued the random lashing. Behind her she heard the sharp slapping noise of a paddle and answering female cries. She gave Patti a break and turned to see the other slave's bound tits, getting shiny and dark in their constriction, bounce and shudder under the paddling. The Housegirl watched each blow arrive with eyes wide and mouth hanging open. The club member stopped the beating momentarily and felt between her spread legs. Angel saw his fingers emerge, glistening with her outpourings, then she turned back to Patti and concentrated on her heaving breasts, bringing her to orgasm several times as she launched a blizzard of hard lashes on their quivering vulnerability.

The leather of the bench was stained dark by Patti's juices as Angel sank her fingers into the flooding quim and twisted them inside the slave, making her heave and wriggle in pleasure. Angel's own cunt ached for attention but she had all night and moved Patti to another bench, over which she had her bend forwards and took a heavy leather paddle to her backside, beating it until it was a pretty, fiery red colour. Then she used the riding crop on it. Patti added her howls to those of the other slave who now had two needles through each nipple and the dungeon became an ever more heated pressure cooker of lust and excitement. At length both dominants gave in to their desires and as the Lodge member stripped off his trousers and lifted his girl's legs so she could wrap them around him while he fucked her, Angel found a dildo and brought herself off standing behind Patti and admiring the tramlines seared into the flesh of the buttocks.

The slave and her current master climaxed together just before Angel herself came and for a moment the dungeon fell silent as everyone recovered.

But Angel was far from sated and as soon as she had recovered her breath she dragged Patti up and attached her wrists to a chain hanging from the ceiling, then she pressed herself against her back, reaching round to squeeze and fondle the heavy breasts, running her hands down the stomach to stroke and rub at the clitoris just enough to drive Patti wild with desire and frustration. She writhed against Angel's body and begged to be made to come. Angel smiled in delight as she felt her breasts rubbed by Patti's back and she revelled in ignoring the woman's desperate pleas for release.

She stepped back and took up the flogger again. Patti craned her head round and cast a look of mingled lust, fear and excitement at her just before the first lash caught her across the shoulders. Her head fell forward and she groaned with pleasure. Angel took her time now, never letting Patti ascend the full heights of orgasm but enjoying herself by marking the pale skin of her back and occasionally letting fly at the heavily striated buttocks, just to wake the slave up a bit.

The member departed with his slave after he had caned her, and as Angel was about to bring herself off again with the dildo while standing in front of Patti, the door of the dungeon opened and another member entered with his girl for the night.

"Please don't let us interrupt you," the man, a florid complexioned sixty year old in Angel's estimation, said. She had no intention of letting them do anything of the sort and while the girl stripped and was put on the medical bench, she spread her legs and began to masturbate in front of Patti, who moaned and writhed in frustration. She came vividly with the sounds of an energetic cunt whipping ringing in her ears. Relaxed and soothed by her orgasm, Angel went back to flogging the almost weeping Patti until the need for more attention to her own cunt finally persuaded her it was time to head for her room.

She slipped her dress back on and led the naked and cuffed Patti on her leash out into the corridor. All the dungeons were in use and the sounds of whips filled the stone passage, with cries of pain and excitement providing a pleasing counterpoint. Back in the main house, the Common Room was emptying and girls in various stages of undress and dishevelment were being led to bedrooms.

Some of the members paused to congratulate Angel on the marks that Patti carried and one donated a pair of nipple clamps which Angel was delighted to apply and had to admit she couldn't think why she hadn't applied them herself. The Housegirl on the member's arm looked relieved while watching Patti suck in her breath and hop as the clamps bit into her tender nubs. But then the member dug into his dinner jacket pocket and produced another pair which he flourished in front of her.

Angel burst into laughter at the look of disappointment on the Housegirl's face and led Patti to her room in high good humour. Once there, she had her lie on the bed while she undressed again and then flung herself onto her, in a rage of urgency, tearing the clamps off. She pressed down onto Patti, feeling the woman's soft skin beneath hers, the swell of her breasts, the insides of her thighs. The slave, with her hands pinned under her back, thrust back up at Angel with her pelvis as Angel's thigh began to rub at her clitoris. Angel covered the slave's mouth with hers and pushed her tongue deep into her mouth, enjoying crushing the woman's softness beneath her. Her hand reached down for a breast and began to maul it and squeeze it. Patti tried to cry out into Angel's mouth and she relished the slave's pain. At times like these, she almost inhabited a submissive's body, even as she was punishing it. She could almost feel the heat and pain and the submission fuelling the helpless flight into orgasm. And she almost lost control and allowed Patti to come, but realised in time what was happening and rolled off. Patti gazed up at her in distress as she smiled back and walked over to her case. She took out a double ended dildo – an item she suspected would be in short supply at The Lodge – and the riding crop she never travelled without. Patti opened her legs avidly as she returned to the bed and Angel slipped the larger and longer shaft into her blossomed cunt. Then she knelt on the bed and lifted Patti's legs until they rested on her shoulders before she shuffled her own thighs apart and fitted the smaller shaft into her own moist and eager cunt. Then she settled herself carefully on the clit rasper, took a firm grip on the riding crop and began to fuck Patti.

Penetrative sex for Angel was never a gentle activity. On the rare occasions when she was a recipient, she demanded that she be battered into submission by a cock. When she was doing the penetration she liked to use the dildo as another tool to punish a slave with. And she did so then; smacking her hips forward, knowing that with her hands behind her and her legs raised, Patti was going to be stuffed to the hilt. Immediately she fetched cry after cry from Patti as she rammed herself into the slave, at the same time feeling her end of the shaft and the rasper wreaking havoc inside her.

"What's the matter, you bitch? Don't want to come now? Is that it? Want me to stop?"

Patti shook her head frantically, tears making her eyes gleam. "No! Please don't stop Mistress!" she managed.

Angel grinned and thrust again, this time adding a flick from the leather keeper of the crop to Patti's breasts.

"Oh! Yes! Thank you, Mistress!" she yelped as her heavy mounds quivered.

Angel thrust and struck again. And again.

Patti came, bouncing frantically under Angel. But Angel hadn't climaxed and even as Patti lay, wrung out beneath her, she battered and struck at her until she too arched rigid at her peak and then fell sideways; satisfied at last.

Patti whispered her thanks as Angel lay, staring up at the ceiling, considering whether or not to subject the woman to any further torment. Reluctantly she concluded that tomorrow was going to be a busy day.

She clipped Patti's wrists together through a link of a chain hanging from a headpost, placed her on her back and fell asleep with her head pillowed on her breasts and her hand between her legs.

Sometime in the night she awoke and in the dark felt the softness of Patti beside her and under her. It sparked the fires of lust once more and after a few minutes of frenzied groping in the moistness of Patti's cunt, Angel heaved herself up and sat astride Patti's face, grinding herself down onto the passionately questing tongue while she twisted and pulled at her nipples.

In the morning Patti helped Angel to wash and shower, soaping her lovingly and eventually squatting down to receive a golden shower from her temporary mistress.

Angel took some time over choosing her clothes and for a very specific purpose chose a short denim skirt and a scoop necked T shirt. After some consultation with Patti – now washed herself but still naked – she decided to leave her bra off, and sauntered down to breakfast. Patti was left to make her way back to the dungeon to retrieve her clothes.

CHAPTER SIX

After breakfast – and a long feel of a delicious brunette Housegirl she hadn't seen before – Angel made her way to the CSL stable. It was her last day and there were a lot of loose ends to tie up.

However, she was surprised to see a T shaped whipping post had been set up in the middle of the yard and tied to it was Patti. Her back already bore some pink criss crossing lines from a flogging.

Angel wasn't quite sure of the protocol but decided that if it were her stable, she wouldn't want a strange dom talking to a slave who was mounted for punishment, so she went to Carlo's office where the Spaniard was drawing up training regimes for his slaves.

"What's Patti's offence?" she asked when he invited her to sit opposite him at the desk.

"She was due here first thing to supervise the feeding and mucking out," he told her.

Angel was immediately contrite. "I'm really sorry, Carlo. She was with me and I didn't know......."

Carlo held up his hand to stop her.

"Don't worry. It was up to her to get back on time. I'll leave her out there for the day and she'll be flogged from time to time."

Angel smiled inwardly as she realised that Patti must have known what her reward was going to be, even as she turned her face up to receive Angel's warm piss.

With the business of Patti's crime out of the way, they got down to business.

"If I take all you've got left, how much discount will you give me?"

"None," Carlo said. "Why should I?"

Angel leaned forward, allowing the low neckline of her shirt to show her cleavage. She knew that although men like Carlo had unlimited access to as many blatantly displayed breasts as they could want; they would always be attracted to ones that weren't entirely on display, and she noticed that Carlo's eyes did flicker downwards for an instant.

"Because you know how much I need them. You know we're cash strapped. And because you know that if Sadia's stable is crushed it won't be good for the arena circuit."

Angel unfolded her arms from in front of her and allowed Carlo to see her erect nipples tenting her shirt. The knowledge that Patti was outside awaiting a further flogging was having an effect.

Carlo smiled and nodded slightly.

"It's true that we need new stables. Competition is good for everyone.......Nice tits by the way."

Angel couldn't help but smile back. Touché, she thought.

Carlo stood up abruptly and went to a cupboard, which, when he opened it, revealed a range of whips all neatly coiled and hanging from hooks.

He took two down and passed one to Angel, then cocked his head in the direction of the yard. Angel took the whip gladly and followed him outside. Patti's head jerked up as she heard their steps and her eyes widened in anticipation.

Angel went to stand on the far side of Patti and stripped off the rubber band that had been keeping it so neatly coiled, as it fell, she could feel the way it was weighted. It was a good one and she appreciated the honour that Carlo was according her. They were going to talk as trainer to trainer.

Carlo swung in the first lash and a flash of excitement ran through Angel as Patti's body arched and twisted slightly. He swung in three more and then named a figure.

Angel took over and laid on four elegantly placed sweeps that left welts wrapping Patti just below her breasts. She knocked six thousand off the figure he had named.

Carlo resumed from his side and wrapped the breasts themselves four times, making Patti rear and twist more urgently. Then he reduced the price by two thousand.

Angel lashed Patti across the buttocks five times and lifted her price by one thousand.

Carlo frowned and went for Patti's thighs, making her hop and lift her legs and begin to yelp. He laid on six before he dropped his price by one more thousand.

Angel did her sums as she went back to Patti's upper back, fetching a guttural cry after each lash. She was concentrating so hard on figures that she scarcely noticed how she almost felt the scorch of the lashes herself as she drank in the sight of the writhing figure in front of her, so naked and lovely in her submission to her masters and mistresses.

"Done!" Angel said and coiled her whip.

They shook hands on the deal.

"Is there any reason why anyone should know I've hired in the rest of the CSL stock?" she asked.

Carlo shrugged. "Not really."

"Then suppose we let it come as a nice surprise!" Angel grinned fiercely.

In the Evening Office of the palace in Bahktar, the light from four standard lamps augmented the moonlight that streamed through the open door and windows. The light wasn't especially needed but the lamps themselves added to the room's attractions. Each light was a naked slavegirl standing erect and absolutely still, legs pressed together, tied at knee and thigh, arms tied behind her. A metal pole ran up behind her and supported a forward protruding bar at crotch height that had a butt plug and a dildo mounted on it as well as a small lamp at the front. This was turned upwards to illuminate the superb tattoos that adorned each girl's torso. At the top was the main light that was shaded so that the girl's head was hidden.

In each corner of the room the motionless, statue-like girls kept vigil. Two of the girls bore tattoos of climbing plants that spiralled around them and were picked out in gentle colours. The two others had mythical creatures picked out on them in reds and blacks, with roaring mouths tattooed on breasts and clawed feet and legs depicted across buttocks.

In the centre of the room was a table, from which two men were eating their supper. They were eating from the bodies of two more girls tied down on their backs to the table, with their arms above their heads. Their navels held humous and from between their spread legs oozed a honey and mustard dressing that had been given extra pungency by having been injected deep into their cunts. Pitta bread and celery lay between their thighs to dip into the dressing and slices of cold meat adorned their breasts.

Even the chairs the men sat on were formed by living girls. In skin tight latex their torsos were upside down in a steel frame and their buttocks and the backs of their thighs formed the cushions of the seats. If the men sat back, they rested against the backs of their calves which were braced by upward-reaching arms of the frames that encased the torsos.

"You don't have to leave, Peter," the Prince of Bakhtar said, sitting back and wiping his lips on the satin-shiny black hair of the girl who knelt beside him, dressed only in a hip length, sheer silk tunic.

"I appreciate that kindness along with all your others to me over the years, Your Highness, but I feel that the squad must learn to fear and obey a new trainer."

The prince nodded. "I suppose you're right. We've punished them pretty well all we can, and for you to return would be something of an anticlimax."

In the weeks following the shock defeat of the Bakhtar team by the Girl Squad, Peter Lang, their trainer had had to consider his position carefully. He had built the team up into one of the most successful on the circuit but now his own slaves would know he was not infallible and the only way the long and harsh punishments they had endured for failing their owner could be put to good effect would be to give them a new trainer who would make them wake their ideas up a bit.

He smiled fondly; the days following the defeat had not been entirely bad; the punishments had been on an epic scale. Up country in the old fort where the slaves were housed, a relentless regime of hanging cages from the battlements at night, each one containing a miserable slave, had been introduced. Others had been staked out in the sun during the day with wet rawhide leathers bound around their breasts.

All had been lashed repeatedly. All had been given to whichever men in Bakhtar wanted them, free of charge, and the stable had echoed to the sounds of whips and screams of pain and release for days on end.

But now it was over and both he and the stable had to move on, but the image of rows of girls staked out on their backs and writhing, with the sun relentlessly tightening the straps on their tits was one he would carry with him for a long time.

And the strangest thing of all was that he knew that, despite all the punishment they could inflict, the slaves would be punishing themselves even more harshly in shame and regret for having let down their owner and trainer. Another reason it was better they had a new trainer and moved on.

The two men rose and took their wine out into the atrium. As was the prince's custom in this area of the palace, he and his guest were naked. Peter appreciated the cool air caressing him as he walked across to the pool that lay at the centre of the atrium and sat on its side, letting his feet dangle in the water and with his thighs wide apart. On the rock in the centre of the pool, some of the mermaids who were playing with each other looked up to see if they were needed. The mass of naked girlflesh, gleaming with water and moonlight as they formed sixty-nines and kissed and caressed each other, looked almost otherworldly as he clicked his fingers and beckoned one across. She swam straight between his legs and then rose up to smoothly engulf his semi tumescent cock in her gentle mouth. She used her hands to keep herself steady in the water and no other part of her – apart from the occasional wisp of wet hair – touched him. Under her gentle ministrations with her tongue, he began to swell and thicken. With one hand he took a sip of his wine, with the other he pressed her more deeply down onto himself. He sighed as he felt her throat caress him and contain him.

Beside him the prince sat down facing the other way and pulled the slave who had knelt beside him during the meal, down between his own thighs and she began to fellate him.

In companionable silence the two men enjoyed the girls until, one after the other they pressed the girls hard down onto them and spilled themselves into their throats.

Peter's mermaid held steady until she was sure he was clean and softening, then she left him, licking her lips, her teeth gleaming briefly in the semi darkness.

It would be hard to tear himself away from this carefully organised depravity, this casually disposed of wealth of compliant and well trained girls. It was pure heaven of a sort. He said so to the prince.

"Well what will you do with yourself if you must leave us? You will not be short of money; I shall see to that."

"Again, you are kindness itself, Your Highness. I'm not sure just yet.....but do you recall that girl we took as a bet once?"

"The one from London? Yes. What happened to her? She was very good, as I recall!"

"I let her go. Got bored with her, Ayesha her name was. I might do the same with another girl – or go and find her again – or both. I don't think I'll stray too far from the arenas though."

The prince laughed aloud. "What man in his right mind would?"

"She's fighting out of the CSL stable now, maybe I'll go and look up Carlo and see how the land lies there."

"Well, you are assured of a warm welcome here at any time. You couldn't have foreseen how good that Countess' stable was going to be, you do understand that I hold you in the highest esteem, Peter?"

"Yes, Your Highness. Thank you."

"And now I think we should go and make music till the early hours to celebrate all our years together!"

The prince stood up and clapped Peter on the shoulder.

"Sounds good to me!" Peter said, standing up with a smile.

The prince was striding back into the Evening Office shouting for servants. He wanted them to open up the Music Room, the place where he played with the almost uncounted complement of females the palace was home to.

And it wasn't even as if the prince had to expend any of his vast wealth on purchasing them. His own people thought it only right and fitting their semi-divine monarch should have all the women he wanted and frequently gave them to him.

The prince turned to him as he entered and he saw that a male servant was waiting to hear how the room was to be prepared. The prince poured more wine.

"We haven't played the drawing pin game for a while, have we?" he said.

There was a desk in the Music Room at which he sometimes worked while his slaves were worked on in their turn. When the drawing pin game was played, at either end of the desk a full packet of drawing pins would be spilled and carefully turned point up.

Each man would select a slave and see how quickly she could gather up the pins using her breasts alone, as he pressed her down onto the desk and then picked out the pins. The first to clear his end of the desk would win.

During a long evening – as this one promised to be – buttocks could also be applied. The music this produced was quite loud; especially if the buttocks had previously been beaten.

"D'you know," Peter said as they settled back to finish their drinks while the servants set the room up and furnished it with a suitable number of slaves. "I can't remember who won the last time we played."

"Peter, is it not part of your own army that has as its motto; 'Who cares who wins'?"

Peter laughed. "Play up, play up and play the game!" he said.

CHAPTER SEVEN

Amelia – number Ninety-seven – knew that the Girl Squad was about to be thrown into an arena for the second time in its history and her heart pounded in excitement at the prospect. To fight and compete and suffer in front of the eager crowds and to please her owner had been her ambition when she had run away from her job as a groom and her master at CSL. And as the anonymous Ninety-seven, kept naked and tongue-ringed, beaten and whipped daily, she was in heaven. The first inkling she and her fellow slaves had that action was imminent was when they were no longer allowed to bed down with their regular partners. Instead, at the end of each day's training, the barracks were filled randomly and the girls were chained into bed with a different partner each night.

At first she missed having Seventy-six to make love to before dropping into deep sleep, but then variety began to be the spice of life and she found that she was looking forward to tasting a different cunt every night, to feeling smaller or bigger tits against her own. Of course, once the games were over she would want Seventy-six back but for now the change was welcome and exciting.

Having spent time with trainers and their stables before engineering her own abduction and enslavement, she understood what Angel was doing; she was reminding each girl of what she was fighting for. When it came to desperate mauls in the arenas, each member of the Girl Squad would know that she was fighting for her lovers as well as her stable's honour, and would fight the harder.

As the girl who had once been Amelia Johnson smiled in bed on the night that Angel returned from wherever she had been, she knew she would have to be carried out of the arena rather than lose any fight or competition. She also gasped in delight as the pretty Chinese girl she had been bedded with, ran her tongue, with its heavy ring, round every crevice and orifice between her legs and buttocks. As they were lying head to toe; eager, excited and happy, Ninety-seven turned her own head and began to lick carefully at the Chinese girl's cunt and then followed the perineum back towards her buttocks. The shapely and satin-smooth thighs parted eagerly for her and she delved deeply with her tongue, savouring the girl's fragrance and the cheeky little hard nub of the clitoris, then the contours of the anus.

While the slaves pleasured each other, at the other side of the stockade in the big house, Angel propped herself up on her elbow and looked down at Sadia. Both women were naked, Sadia lay on her back, her arms flung up above her head, her hands still gripping the headboard of the bed, as they had during her orgasm.

At the foot of the bed, still bound with her face buried in the quilt and her hands behind her and her bottom raised, the slave they had been caning until urgency overtook them, remained, available and ready for whatever her owners chose to do with her.

In the lamplight, Angel looked down at Sadia's still-heaving breasts, the nipple rings gleaming in the light. Between her carelessly spread legs, the metal tag and the rings rested against the engorged flesh of her sex.

"Oh, my lady!" she sighed eventually.

"Oh, come now! It's not that bad! And think of it this way; what you're looking at is twenty brand new, beautiful slaves. All yours to train up and enjoy!"

Angel lay down beside her, still on her side so that she could reach out and gently lift one of the nipple rings. Her mouth still tasted of Sadia's cunt juice mixed with the acrid taste of the metal she hadn't been able to avoid getting into her mouth when she lapped and licked deep into the cunt. It had been just as she had imagined.

"It's not really ownership, it's just a contract that I'll accompany him at club events."

"All the same...." Angel grumbled. She was perfectly used to having to share her lady with someone else, she knew Sadia enjoyed shagging a man from time to time. But to have her nose literally rubbed in it was hard to take.

"Oh, come on Angel! I'm the one wearing the damn things! And believe me they do some fabulous things to the slaves they've got there. You should come along one day!"

Angel just grunted and rolled onto her back. Sadia turned onto her side and put her hand between her legs.

"Let's cane this bitch some more. And this time we'll put her head between those gorgeous legs of yours and she can lick you out while I beat her."

Angel had to admit it was a pleasing prospect. And at least wearing the rings didn't seem to have altered Sadia's appetites in any way. She sat up and crawled to the bottom of the bed, then manoeuvred herself until she was sitting with her legs on either side of the slave. Then she lifted the hooded head and wriggled closer until her cunt was touching the slave's lips. Immediately her tongue came out and began to lick and explore blindly.

Sadia stood at one side of the bed, swishing a cane.

"Ready?" she asked.

"Ready!"

Sadia swung the cane in hard and the slave jumped in shock, her cry fanning Angel's lust-swollen lips delightfully. She put her head back and closed her eyes the better to savour the full sensual experience, gripping the hood and pressing the head to her groin.

"Harder, my lady!"

Sadia was only too glad to comply and Angel's heart leapt at the sound of the cane smacking into the slave's buttocks.

The training became even more rigorous. Amelia did her best to cope with the extra demands it made on her as she admired the way the regime had changed her body. She was actually more curvaceous now that some fat had been trimmed off round her waist and the hard exercise had left her limbs well shaped without being overly sinewy. The increase in her pectoral strength had helped her breasts which retained their pretty uptilted shape, but were now more prominent. Her bottom was higher, tighter and more pert. In short she felt more womanly than ever before. The constantly worn marks of her owner's whips only added to her pride in her attractiveness.

And loving the bodies of her sisters and being loved by them only increased her sense of her femininity. But running through her mind, and the minds of most of the slaves, she reckoned, was that the arenas meant men! The Girl Squad had some male guards and sometimes they would play with and fuck the slaves. But at an arena, they all knew that in the evenings after the games, they would be hired out for guests to play with in dungeons and there was only one thing a slavegirl needed after a thorough beating and suspension or bondage and that was a good hard cock.

On some evenings the guards – male and female - would look in on the barracks before they came to chain them all down for the night and lob in a handful of dildos and vibrators, then stand and watch the cat fights as the desperate girls fought each other for the right to be first to masturbate. Amelia felt no shame about having thrown herself into the naked wriggling mass on the floor; only pride when she managed to bring an expensive vibrator back for Seventy-six.

She knew that Angel would not allow any more of that before the games. In fact it might well be that they would not be allowed to sleep with anyone at all for several nights before the games. The slaves needed to get to the arena as frustrated and horny as it was possible to get them.

They ran farther and were whipped to ever greater speeds. They were harnessed and drilled mercilessly in dressage. They ran the chariots around the arena until they were dizzy. They boxed, wrestled and fought with whips until girls collapsed in exhaustion. They were even driven on under the sweltering mid day sun, something that had never happened before and Amelia could only assume that they were destined for somewhere hot.

The solitary confinement pits at the side of the training ground stood empty, because punishments were handed out in the form of summary whippings at the posts. The days passed in a seemingly endless series of painful and exhausting training sessions that left the slaves prone, sweat-streaked, bruised, welted and gasping for breath.

Through the mass of prostrate, naked girls strode Angel and the Countess de Groncourt. Always Angel wore her shining boots and her pressed jodhpurs with a crisp white shirt against which her magnificent breasts swelled. Beside her the dark haired countess would stroll; a wide brimmed sun hat on her head and a fabulously expensive sundress to mid calf, enclosing her graceful figure. Occasionally Angel would prod a gasping slave with her riding crop and pass comment to one of the guards.

One day they had spent the morning practising kicks. One slave stood with a plastic shield held at chest height while another had to kick it hard from standing directly in front of her. Each high kick had to be hard and fast. They were expected to launch at least thirty in a minute. Angel stood by with a stopwatch as the rate of kicking inevitably declined as the girls tired. Amelia's eyes stung as sweat streamed into them, her hair clung maddeningly to her face and try as she might, each time her kicking foot touched the ground and she tried to raise it again, it moved more and more slowly. She gritted her teeth and screamed with effort as the minute wore on and her muscles cramped and protested.

The guards passed behind the row of high-kicking girls and 'helped' by flicking with their whips between their legs as they delivered the kicks.

At last Angel blew her whistle and the kickers collapsed gratefully; Amelia felt sure her heart would burst. But slowly her breathing came back under control and she sat up to take a swig of water from a tin jug that was being passed around.

"Not too bad!" Angel called out. "Swap places now!"

For a blessed minute she was able to just stand and hold the shield while another girl tried desperately to pump one leg up and down, delivering kicks up on tip toe with her other leg, then kicking leg down, touch the ground, kick again.

Amelia grinned fiercely as she saw the girl's gathering exhaustion and felt the blows lessen and slow as the minute wore on. She rallied a bit as a guard snapped his whip up into her cunt a few times but by the end she was screaming with effort and hardly able to stand any more.

Once again there was a short rest and the guards conferred with Angel, then she called out a few numbers and the luckless slaves – guilty of not having tried their hardest were dragged to the posts and given fifty lashes each.

Amelia sat and watched the deliciously writhing forms and listened to the exciting sounds of the whips. Grimly she concentrated on maintaining the correct posture for witnessing punishments. She sat with her knees raised and parted, her wrists resting on the knees. Woe betide any girl found playing with herself while sentence was carried out. For the wretches concerned, things got worse. Usually they were left at the posts after their punishments and the male guards could be relied on not to pass by a well flogged female desperate for relief.

On this day, Angel had them taken straight down and ordered a run before any break for food would be taken.

Amelia was about to struggle to her feet when the shadow of the countess fell across her and she squinted up.

"Oh look! It's Ninety-seven!" her owner said. "She was my talisman at Bakhtar!"

It had been the proudest moment of Amelia's life when she had been dragged, semi conscious from the arena, and laid on a bed. The Countess had vowed to taste her cunt while she was still battered and bruised from the arena. 'The Taste of Victory' she had said before the games started. And true to her word she had bent down, opened Amelia's legs and gently licked right inside her cunt. Then she had straightened up, way too soon for Amelia's liking, and declared that the taste of victory was sweat. There had been general laughter and Angel had agreed heartily with her mistress. The crowd of hangers-on and friends had turned back to their drinks and Amelia had been dragged away back to the barracks.

Now the countess smiled down at her.

"D'you think she might be for these games?"

"It'll take more than that, my lady!" Angel said sourly and the countess took her arm and chided her for being so churlish.

The two moved off but Amelia heard Angel give orders that the next two days would be rest and light exercise.

Her heart leaped. The time was nearly at hand again.

Angel surpassed herself that night. As Amelia had feared, sex was prohibited but Angel went farther than that. The girls were put into the small double beds as normal but were chained with their wrist cuffs fastened behind their backs and with their ankle cuffs fastened together as well. Placed head to toe in each bed, they slept together, naked and immobile. Totally frustrated. It was far, far worse than being made to sleep alone, and Angel knew it. Exhaustion came to their aid but in the morning, the mood in the barracks was black indeed.

After a day's rest and just light sparring, the frustration was worse but again sleep rescued them and Amelia was lost in admiration. Angel had judged it to perfection. They slept because of exhaustion and so were rested, but were furious and snarling, keen to do battle and experience the blitz of pain and pleasure the arena would provide.

A second day of rest and light training passed slowly, the guards were everywhere now, keeping careful watch on hands in case they strayed between legs. But the discipline held.

Amelia was astonished by how easily she fell asleep that night despite an almost physical ache from her neglected cunt.

The next morning as the squad trooped onto the training ground once they had been fed, they saw two large trucks parked and everyone knew that they were on the move.

Each truck had four benches running the length of its back. The slaves were seated with their legs slightly parted and their ankle cuffs chained tightly to the floor. Their wrists were cuffed together and put between their knees before being chained down tightly as well.

Once all the benches were full the doors were slammed and they sat in darkness until their eyes adjusted. There were small vents at the tops of the van's sides and, as Amelia glanced around she saw Seventy-six smiling at her from the far side and they exchanged air kisses.

Beside her the dark haired girl she had slept with chastely for the previous night wriggled slightly on her seat, touching thighs with her. They too exchanged smiles and the girl kissed Amelia's shoulder. Suddenly all around her were the sounds of bottoms quietly being wriggled and some soft giggles.

When the truck's engine started and it moved off, the shuffling and fidgeting got worse and Amelia realised her own nipples were achingly hard. They were on their way and after only a few miles the truck was filled with the pungent fragrance of female excitement.

After what seemed like a long time the truck began to bounce as if it were going over grass, then it stopped for a moment and men's voices could be heard shouting. There was a clanging of metal and then the truck moved forward slowly and climbed a steep gradient. The engine's growl echoed and then died. There were more voices and noises from outside, by the wheels it seemed to Amelia. Then at last the doors were thrown open and they could see that the trucks had been driven into a cavernous cargo plane.

Angel hoisted herself up into the truck, followed by several men who stood and admired the scenery.

"Take your pick and be quick about it! I want this plane out of here fast, we're running late as it is."

Amelia understood perfectly well. As always when transporting hundreds of naked women around, there was a price to pay for their discreet passage out of and into various countries. And what was the point of having hundreds of naked females if they weren't used to pay that very price? Amelia sat up as the men began to prowl along the lines, examining the goods. She pushed her breasts out enticingly and she wasn't the only one. Every girl on the truck was wiggling and pouting and inviting the men in any way she could. The men themselves laughed and exchanged comments that Amelia couldn't understand, but could guess at the meaning of perfectly well.

Suddenly one man stopped in front of her and reached down. She watched his brown, work-calloused hand touch the lightly tanned skin of her breast and a shiver of pleasure ran down her. He squeezed her flesh hard and she shuddered in masochistic excitement. Then he flicked her uptilted nipples one after the other, smiled at her as they hardened and called out to a guard who came and unfastened her chains.

Amelia stood up, well aware of the envious glances from either side of her, and followed the man to the open doors at the back of the truck. He jumped down and lifted her down courteously after him. But that was the last of any courtesy.

He held her close with one hand and the other dived unceremoniously between her naked thighs. Amelia had expected no less and had already spread them wide for him. His thick fingers slid up into her and she moaned in appreciation, resting her head against his sweat-redolent shirt. He called out to his mates as he twisted and swirled his fingers inside her and there was more coarse laughter. She could guess the girls they had chosen were being called whores and sluts as they opened their legs so easily and welcomed in any man who wanted them. Amelia was perfectly happy with that description. Proud of it even.

She slid her hand down between their bodies and ran her looped fingers up and down the long and thick bulge of his cock inside his work trousers. He smiled down fiercely and pushed her away just enough to free his hand from her cunt and instead grip her breasts and twist her rock hard nipples.

After only a few seconds though, he had had enough of feeling her up and spun her around to face the side of the fuselage. She reached out and grasped the horizontal steel bars that ran between the thick stanchions, then thrust her hips back at him and arched her back prettily. She knew her backside was good and her legs too, so it was no surprise that when she looked over her shoulder she saw a truly impressive length of cock being freed from his trousers. All along the fuselage there were girls being put to use and Angel walked up and down behind the men. She stopped by Amelia's man and reached down to give his shaft a squeeze or two and peel back the foreskin.

"That should stuff her to the hilt!" she said and slapped him on the shoulder before moving on.

Amelia felt the broad dome lodge itself at her entrance and then be rammed into her. She braced herself to withstand the thrust and cried out in pleasure as she felt her sheath stimulated up its entire length.

"Come on, lads!" Amelia heard Angel's voice echo from the far end of the fuselage. "Fuck my bitches good and hard and then get 'em back in the truck. They've got a living to earn!"

Amelia's man, even if he didn't speak English seemed to gather the gist of what was said and delivered a fuck that was as hard and as fulfilling as anything she had had in the recent past. His pelvis slapped against her buttocks time and again and the ecstasy that engulfed her from her cunt made her scream with relief. The fact that he used his huge hands to maul her breasts just as she was about to drown in overload nearly brought her to her knees as she came and then came again and finally came one last, mind blowing time as he spurted himself into her and pulled out. She tottered forwards and rested her forehead on the cool steel in the wake of the fuck but as she slid gently to her knees, her hair was grabbed and she was turned around. His still semi-tumescent cock was before her, gleaming with his spunk and her discharge. She opened her mouth without a qualm and licked him clean, taking long, luxurious licks, savouring every swallow of the mingled juices.

"Load 'em back in now, boys!" Angel shouted as presumably the final coupling had been completed. Amelia and the others from her truck were picked up bodily and thrust back then chained back down. On either side of her, Amelia could see her sisters' eyes devouring the sight of the shiny trails on the insides of her thighs. She grinned back at them and licked her lips lasciviously.

When the aircrew came to take their payment, Amelia was pleased that Seventy-six was one of those chosen.

CHAPTER EIGHT

The flight was a long one. In relays the slaves were taken out to use the toilets and be fed, then put back. They slept as best they could as the engines droned thunderously and then again they were taken out, watered, fed and put back. With no portholes, it was impossible to gauge the time they were airborne and impossible to estimate whether they were flying with or against the sun.

But at long last they felt the thump of the landing gear going down and the plane lurched as it began its approach. Amelia's heart thundered in her chest and she could see her own mingled anxiety and excitement mirrored in her sisters' eyes as they tensed themselves for the landing. There was another thump as the wheels hit tarmac and then the engines screamed and they were thrown forwards as the brakes were applied. Finally there was the rumble of taxiing which itself died away and the plane was stationary at last. For good or ill; they had arrived at the next games.

The first thing that hit them was the heat. As the plane's cargo doors opened it hit them as an almost physical force, even though it appeared to be early evening. By the time the trucks had been reversed out and the customs and ground staff had been paid – Amelia was passed over in favour of her big breasted neighbour, the girl she had slept beside the night before their departure – all the slaves had a slick of sweat on their skins that gleamed in the last of the daylight. The speed with which the sun set was confirmation, if any were needed, that they were near the equator. To begin with the trucks drove along smooth roads but before too long they seemed to turn onto rougher roads and the girls were thrown this way and that against each other until they came to a final halt.

For a long time they were left in the dark, the heat building to almost unbearable levels but at last the doors were flung open and slightly less hot night air wafted in, bringing with it scents that were exotic and strange and the noises of a forest alive with nocturnal life.

The squad huddled together as they were freed and lifted down. Being naked slaves in familiar territory was one thing, being naked, tired and frightened in a strange country was entirely different. It was obvious that they were much farther from home than they had been in Bakhtar. Men went about their business around them, predominantly with dark skins and high cheek bones with bandannas wrapped around their heads. Indonesia or the Philippines was her best guess and as she shook sweat off her face, she hoped Angel had negotiated a couple of days' acclimatisation.

She needn't have worried. They were housed in a timber stockade that had roofed shelter provided all round its perimeter, the steeply slanting roof coming downwards towards the open ground in the centre. Under the roof, there was simply a long line of shackles to which the slaves were chained with enough slack to lie comfortably on the cots provided but not enough to allow for any bed hopping. Their hands were clipped to their collars when it was at last time for sleep.

The next day dawned gloriously clear and warm, free of the previous night's humidity. Breakfast was served by beautiful, delicately featured girls in brightly coloured sarongs to the slaves who sat at one long table in the middle of the compound. Amelia noticed that guards patrolled the tops of the stockade walls on walkways set just below the tops of the walls and on their outsides. She knew enough to know that they weren't there to stop the slaves escaping; they were all too well trained now and looking forward to everything the games could throw at them. It was far more likely they were there to protect them from marauding local males.

For the whole of that day they were free to wander, sit in the shade, take showers and groom each other as the official grooms tended to the elite solo fighters. To maintain discipline however, one girl was accused of trying to feel another's cunt and was mounted facing the stockade wall and given fifty lashes, then left to bake in the sun for a while.

In the late afternoon it rained. Amelia had never seen anything like the downpour that engulfed the site. The rain hammered down with such force that it threw up a mist about a foot high off the ground. It went on for over an hour as the naked girls sheltered under the roof and began to shiver as the temperature dropped. They huddled together for warmth and watched as the compound became a shallow lake. Then the rain stopped and almost immediately the sun came out, raising steam from the standing water and turning the water into thick mud if anyone tried to walk outside. Amelia watched all this in trepidation. If this was to be typical, she hoped that Angel and Sadia were watching as carefully as she was. The humidity began to soar and just as she was wringing sweat out of her hair again, another truck arrived and disgorged a batch of CSL slaves.

As soon as Amelia saw the big crates being slid out of the back of the truck, she knew what she was looking at. Each one contained a hog tied slave and as they were stacked on the wet ground, she caught sight of Sam's flame red hair. Leaving the group of girls she had been standing with she managed to get closer to the rear of the truck and saw Legs, Blackie and Rose, then watched as Purdy was unloaded and stacked, then

Cherry and finally Lucky. The men handling the crates were covered in red mud almost to their knees and the slaves in the bottom crates were also red almost to their necks.

When all the crates were unloaded, Tony jumped down from the truck, sending up a wave of more red mud, and as the truck reversed out and the gates closed after it, he began to open the crates while Eve helped him.

A strange mixture of emotions filled her as she watched them rub circulation back into cramped limbs until the slaves could hobble and then walk properly towards the only walled building under the roof which was where the grooms and the solo fighters were quartered. Angel, Sadia and Doctor Hooper, the new vet who had joined them only a matter of days before, stepped through a wicket gate set in one of the tall, main gates and Amelia listened eagerly to the conversation.

"All arrived safely?" Angel asked as Eve led Rose round on her tongue ring to get the last of the stiffness out of her.

Doctor Hooper, tall, willowy and with thick mousy hair, stepped forward and went to where the others had been tethered to the uprights that supported the roof. She began running her hands over them, slapping their flanks and smacking their buttocks.

"Good stock!" she crowed like a child in a sweetshop, moving swiftly on from slave to slave. "Excellent tone and musculature. I'd heard CSL had good slaveflesh, but these are real beauties!"

"You should see the others," Sadia told her. "These are comparatively unblooded. But when you see Blondie –"

Amelia saw Angel lay a hand on Sadia's arm and jerk her head in the Squad's direction. Sadia looked from her trainer to her slaves.

"So what?" she asked. "Most of them probably never spoke English in any case. And they'll get on with their jobs no matter who they're put in against! Relax, Angel."

Amelia looked on thoughtfully as all three women fussed over the bought in stock and made sure it was stabled properly.

She ran over in her mind the slaves she had seen. Sadia was right, it was the entire lightweight end of the CSL catalogue – except for Cherry, who was an elegant whip dueller and runner but wasn't much used in the rougher, endurance and strength events. So why had Angel spent......Amelia did a few rough calculations and would have whistled had she been able to...... why had Angel spent so much on lightweight and inexperienced stock when there were Ayesha, Tigre, Ox, Trouble, Beast and the others available. Not to mention Blondie herself. If they were all available then why......? Her thoughts stopped in their tracks. Maybe they weren't available. She knew that the Owners' Council had decreed a few months back that no more than two games should take place simultaneously anywhere in the world. And it was very rare that dates coincided at all.......and that meant........

She was so deep in consideration of the implications that she didn't notice Angel, Sadia, the vet, Tony and Eve walking across to take a look at the Squad. When she looked up, it was to look straight into the astonished gaze of Eve.

Of course she had known it was bound to happen and at least now, with one successful games under their belts, Angel and Sadia couldn't possibly think she was spying for CSL or up to anything clandestine.

"Oh my God!" Eve squeaked. "It's Amelia!"

She rushed up and hugged her. "We were so worried about you! But Brian said you'd be okay, said you knew what you were doing! Wait till I tell the others you're a fully trained arena slave!"

Thank you, Brian, was all Amelia could think. He had seen her at the Bakhtar games but had kept her secret.

"You know this one!?" Angel asked sharply as Tony pulled Eve off and smacked her bottom hard to calm her down.

"Yeah, she used to be a part time groom and subbed to Brian Holden back home," he told her.

Amelia tried to look Angel in the eye but couldn't. She wasn't clear why not, it wasn't as though she had done anything wrong and she had had to hide her identity to be treated as the slave she desperately wanted to be.

Sadia came to her rescue and took her chin in her hand and tilted her face up, smiling at her.

"You know, she just might be our talisman after all," she mused. "Did she spar with the others – Ayesha, Blondie, Ox, Jet?"

"Yeah, all of them," Tony confirmed.

"Pity there's only one of her!" Angel said. "Still, she's a weapon they don't know we've got! When we sort out the final list of entrants for each event, we'll see how much advantage we can get."

The group turned and moved off, Eve giving her a little wave as she left. Amelia breathed out and glanced around. Some of the others – ones who must have understood English were staring at her in awe. Seventy-six was one of them. She came across and put her arm round her shoulders, kissing her long and ardently; risking a flogging. Amelia returned the kiss. At long last her secret was out and it was alright. She was accepted as a simple slave – but one with a value beyond her purchase price. Seventy-six was reiterating her claim on her in front of the others and Amelia felt truly at home.

There was a lot to think about though. It was clear that their opposition had hired in all the rest of the CSL stock and that meant that the Girl Squad was up against the toughest fighters on the circuit. Obviously Angel had bought in what she could to fight back with but she would need all the help Amelia could give her to avoid the Squad being crushed.

Josef came for her at dusk the following day. It had been a tedious day with all the girls' hands chained behind their backs to prevent any sexual contact. They had all recovered from the journey and were getting restive. Some of them discovered that if they jammed themselves up behind their lovers, the fingers of the girl in front could just about frot the clitoris of the girl behind. It was relief of a sort but Amelia found that the small orgasm she got left her even more bad tempered and out of sorts.

Even her admiration for the way Angel manipulated her squad couldn't improve her mood as she stared out at the afternoon downpour.

If the arena wasn't roofed, then some of the events would degenerate into mud wrestling. She had to admit that that wasn't such a bad thought. She enjoyed the feel of a slick body squirming against hers and she knew how much the spectators enjoyed the sight of mass humiliation. And that was the main thing.

Josef found her with Seventy-six trying to frig her and cheerfully wielded his strap to chase her away. He had had to wield it virtually constantly as he passed through the stockade, to break up couples. He was a big man with black curly hair who was popular with the slaves. He had a hard whip hand and a big cock and was fond of using both. He was strict without being vicious and was cheerful even when dishing out the harshest discipline. He shooed Seventy-six away, bent slightly and simply threw Amelia over his shoulder, then he made his way out, one hand on her bottom to steady her.

CHAPTER NINE

Amelia's head bumped and jerked against Josef's back as he carried her, nevertheless she tried to look around her. Outside their stockade, as he marched through the ankle deep mud, Josef passed alongside the arena. It had a concrete base up to about twenty feet and from then upwards was made of wood. However, it seemed every bit as big as any she had seen before, and she noted that it seemed to be open roofed. Mud wrestling it was then!

They went past another stockade like the one they were being held in and she assumed that that was where the opposition were being quartered. If she was right in her assumption about who the Orange team had hired in, then many of her old charges from CSL and perhaps even her ex-master would be there.

Josef marched on. Now they went past another wooden building, it was long and its roofs sloped upwards over what was obviously terracing on either side of the wide central valley. Amelia reckoned it was where the pens would be. Beyond that was a large clearing in the forest surrounded by grandstands. That looked like a dressage ring or pony track, or both. The owner's house was obvious, stone built and enormous, it was guarded by swarthy men holding long Malacca canes who greeted Josef quite calmly as he passed. In the world of the arenas, a man carrying a naked and bound woman over his shoulder was nothing to remark on. Then they came to a low building with a veranda running the length of its front.

Josef climbed the steps and then heaved her down back onto her feet, she tottered for a moment and looked around her while she got her balance back. Over to her right one of the host's household slaves had been bent over the railings. She was naked apart from white, high-heeled strappy sandals. Her legs were parted and tied at the ankles to the wooden uprights. Her upper body was dimly visible on the other side of the railings, where, Amelia guessed, her wrists were tied to her ankles. A riding crop jutted out jauntily from between her shapely thighs, just below her flogged buttocks. It had been stuck into her vagina in the wake of a good flogging and Amelia's heart went out to the girl. She would be desperately clenching her inner muscles on the shaft, trying for any release from the excitement the beating had lit inside her. In vain of course. But for Tony, sitting in a swing chair against the house wall just behind and along from the slave, her wriggling and clenching would be fun to watch. He was dressed only in shorts and waved at her cheerfully when she looked at him. She didn't know how to respond and instead looked along the veranda. On the other side of the door into the house was a table which was lit by a lamp hung from Eve.

Tony had been busy with his famous rope skills and had hung his sub up in a hog tie. Her wide eyes stared anxiously into the darkness above the ball gag that stretched her jaws. Her long, shiny black hair had been plaited and was tied to a rope that Amelia guessed was connected to an anal hook, keeping her back arched. From between thick bands of rope her breasts managed to squeeze out and chains running from nipple clamps ran down to an oil lamp, a third supporting chain ran down from a clit clamp. Eve was protected from the heat by the lamp's steel lid, but Amelia could imagine the chains might get a bit warm.

On the table was a collection of clip boards, sheets with numbers and schematics of the arena and the pony track, together with lists of events; mostly the competitors' numbers hadn't been filled in. The pens, pencils, highlighters and other implements were stored in the upturned cunt of an ankle suspended slave held tight against the wall of the house behind the table. Amelia's belly melted and she tried to rub her thighs together. She adored the way the arenas exploited every inch of the available girlflesh for its own – and the public's – entertainment. There were very few women who were exempt and one of them was on the sofa at the left hand end of the veranda.

Sadia reclined with one leg on the floor and other raised onto the cushion beside her. She had been wearing a wrap which was now thrown wide open and with her dark head tipped back, she was gently playing with her own ringed nipples while between her legs, another slave was busily tonguing her. Amelia was surprised by the rings. She had been played with up at the big house only a week or two before and there had definitely not been rings then. Amelia licked her lips fondly in recollection. There was the hollow noise of heels on the wooden floor of the house and Angel appeared in the doorway. She held a tall glass with a drink and ice cubes in it. She used a finger to stir it and sucked it dry between her full lips as Amelia looked at her in total admiration. Her thick blonde hair was loosely tied back in the heat and she wore a simple white shirt dress. It was loose above her waist but even so, Amelia could see her unfettered breasts swing and tremble against it as she walked. Below the belt it was a tight and short skirt that left the long tanned thighs naked almost to their tops. Amelia's heart skipped a beat at the thought of being allowed to kneel and explore beneath it. The fragrant and silky-soft lips of the cunt were so close!

"Thanks for bringing it, Josef. You can leave it there," Angel said.

Josef's heavy tread receded into the distance and for a moment the only sound was Sadia groaning in pleasure and the endless chirruping and calling from the forest.

Angel turned slightly towards Tony.

"It's odd to think of them having names. What did you say this one's was?" she asked.

"Amelia," Tony told her and Amelia found herself blinking as if her name being spoken had woken her up.

"Amelia," Angel repeated, seeming to taste the name. "Well come over here and.....oh, of course you can't speak. But you can understand and nod or shake your head, can't you?" She said the last words in exaggeratedly slow fashion, as if talking to a child. Amelia nodded and followed the spectacular buttocks, joggling seductively under the tight skirt, over to the table. Tony came and joined them.

Over on her sofa, Sadia shifted her hips a little farther forwards and pushed the slave's head further down.

"I'll just have her rim me for a bit and then I'll join you," she called over. Angel smiled and shook her head in mock frustration.

"Now.......Amelia," Angel said. "The Orange mob together with persons unknown, we suspect, have hired in every big hitter CSL's got. I've hired in what's left and we've got to make the best of things. Anything that isn't a massacre will be a win of sorts. Understand?"

Amelia nodded again. Her mind was racing now and it wasn't a welcome feeling. She loved being just a body to be placed where others wanted it for their pleasure. To be thrust back into the world of trainers and their concerns was not at all what she desired, and yet part of her was responding. She knew both CSL and the Girl Squad intimately. No one else here did. She felt the old spark that had burned when she and

Brian and Carlo had sat up late with clients, deciding how best to dispose of the slaves, suddenly re-ignite despite herself.

Angel took a clipboard and pointed to a list of events under Day One.

"They only flew their bitches in today so they won't be using them for dressage on the first evening. So let's start with the first full day." Suddenly she threw the board down in frustration. "I can't believe I'm doing this! Trying to talk sense to a cunt on legs! She's just whip fodder for Chrissake......She probably can't understand a word I'm bloody saying!"

Part of Amelia hoped that she would send her back to the stockade. She didn't want this any more than Angel did. On the other hand part of her raged at the woman's stupidity. She could help the squad!

Tony moved round to stand behind her and unclipped her wrists.

"She's no fool, Angel. Trust her," he said quietly.

Sadia sauntered up behind Angel, fastening the belt on her wrap and put an arm round Angel's shoulders. Angel shrugged and turned back to the table, wrenching a pen out of its cunt holder. A gag-muffled grunt came from beneath the table.

"Right! First off we've got a whip melee in the arena. Twenty squaddies on each team. I'm going to put Thirty-three, Nineteen, Seventeen, Two and Forty-eight in with

Cherry, Sam, Lucky and Purdy, then make up the rest with these....." She pointed at a list and Amelia ran her eyes over it.

She thought of who the Orange team would put in; Ox, Trouble, Fiji, Ayesha......they probably wouldn't put Blondie in this early.......They didn't need to.

Suddenly she swept some of the sheets aside and picked up the schedule for Day Two.

She put the sheet next to Day One and pointed to the contests in the pens and the racing. Then she pointed to the CSL names. She grabbed a pen and circled some Girl Squad numbers and drew an arrow from them to the events in the arena.

"What the hell's it doing?" Angel demanded.

"Wait!" Sadia ordered. Amelia's brain was racing and she didn't hear the imperious tone nor see Angel's lips tighten in anger.

On Day Two she began to scribble names against the racing and solo whip duelling. Then she moved on to the chariots, her hand struggling to keep up with her thoughts. The Orange team would expect the Girl Squad to put up their best against the CSL talent and that meant they thought they would deploy the talent that they, the Girl Squad, had hired in. Amelia was setting out to avoid those confrontations at all costs. She knew there was talent in Sadia's stable, and she knew that there were surprises in the younger CSL members.

Let the Orange team win the melees in the arena - perhaps. Let them win the log pulling. Let them think they could walk away with the studded whip duels. Let them think the pursuit running was theirs for the taking.

She defied convention and scribbled in the CSL girls for contests in the pens and not the arenas. There they could knock the heart out of the Orange squad in the boxing, the wrestling and the whip duelling. In the pens a girl could take a lot more punishment going down to defeat than in the arena. There, once she was down, the referees scored against her immediately and she was out of it. In the pens, the crowd liked a good slow show and defeat was longer in coming.

She piled on the possible problems for the Orange team by adding in those Girl Squad members that could more than hold their own. The crowds would demand heavier punishments for slaves who didn't appear to put up a good fight in the pens than in the arenas. The thumbs would stay down until the tally went up to forty, fifty or more lashes sometimes. That would slow them down for assault course running and log pulling on Day Two. With luck it might mean the withdrawal of some chariot racers.

"You're suggesting we pile on the pressure where we can and let them win what they're going to anyway?" Tony asked as her hand flew from list to list.

Amelia nodded. Angel leaned across her and pointed to Ninety-two; a big Siberian girl who had been brought in on the same truck as Amelia when she first arrived at the stable.

"She's good. We'll put her in for the studded whips."

Amelia nodded assent, trying to ignore the way Angel's breasts shifted and swung as she leaned forwards. She concentrated and then put her own number down for the studded whips. Then drew a line to Blondie.

"You sure, Amelia? I mean yes, they're bound to play Blondie there. But why you?" Tony asked. Amelia shrugged helplessly, she had had an idea but it didn't conform to a nod or shake of the head reply.

"But you and Seventy-six are a good bet for at least a couple of two-in-hand races. But not if you're cut to ribbons by her!" Tony protested.

Amelia drew the line again, firmly.

"Hang on," Angel said, looking suddenly thoughtful. "She's being a very definite little bitch." She put a hand on Amelia's shoulder and turned her to look at her. "Do you know something we don't?"

Amelia nodded hard. She wasn't a hundred percent sure but she knew the big blonde as well as anyone. And she knew Carlo too. Angel looked at her for a second more and Amelia got the impression that she understood what it was that Amelia knew.

As it turned out it was a long night.

Once they accepted her strategy, they made the best selection they could for the pens. Then they turned to the arenas and tried to restrict the probable Orange victories. They had to guess which slaves the opposition would put up but it was odds on they'd use what they'd paid so heavily for, in the arenas, so with Amelia's knowledge to complement and fine tune Angel's and Tony's they refined their selection of 'the best of the rest' of the Girl Squad. And Angel had come up with some novel strategies to complement the selection of competitors. Amelia was relieved because it would have taken her hours to write it all out.

But at the end, when Eve had wriggled and cried out above them, making the light dance and flicker and Tony had taken the lamp down, the consensus was that they'd sacrificed as little as possible while giving themselves a fighting chance. The younger CSL cohort would get a chance to shine against Orange squad opposition instead of competing with fighters they already knew. It could be the making of them.

Angel summed it up as Josef clumped back up the steps and Tony clipped Amelia's wrists together again.

"Downhill and with a following wind, we've got a chance of making the third day a real contest."

Just as Josef stepped off the veranda, Amelia heard the sound of the crop being plied on the long suffering girl tied to the railing. It should have filled her with envy, but her mind was still racing and wouldn't stop.

Had they made the best use of the American blonde; number Eighty-four? Was Sam, Purdy, Legs, Sixty-four and Thirteen the best team for the pursuit running?

Even when Josef used the hand he was steadying her with on his shoulder, to feel between her legs, it took him a few moments to moisten her.

When he put her down by the building that housed the pens and shoved her to her knees, she was grateful to be put back in her rightful place. A place where obedience was all and she was just a slaveslut. Josef's cock reared in front of her face as he freed it from his trousers. The light was dim, just some low powered lamps shining from the walls of the pens and some fitful moonlight but she could see the broad dome of his helm glistening, beckoning to her lips and her tongue.

But this could not be a long and sensual fellation. Sexual contact with any of the girls prior to the games was forbidden and she knew that Josef was taking a big risk; in fact she was flattered that carrying her had inflamed him this much.

He reached forwards and took her hair. She just had time to open her mouth wide enough and then he had stuffed himself fully inside. She was too well trained to gag and kept her throat relaxed, loving how his shaft filled every inch of her and touched her so deep inside. She was looking forward to being allowed to make love to Seventy –six again but the next few days of mainly male use was to be savoured nonetheless.

Having pulled her so violently against him that her nose was tickled by his pubes, Josef sighed in relief at having his cock in a woman again and allowed his grip to slacken enough to let Amelia work her mouth backwards and forwards along the hard, ribbed shaft under its smooth skin, his helm still shafting her throat at maximum penetration. However, he couldn't risk discovery and in only a few moments was fucking her face with all his strength, anxious to spill his load and get on with delivering her. Amelia knew better than to try and fight the battering she was taking as he plunged in and out. She let herself be controlled by the hands in her hair and enjoyed the feeling of being used so carelessly. The feel of his cock travelling in and out of her mouth, the feel of the head in her throat, the wait for his explosion and the strength of his control, all conspired to ignite her own loins again and by the time she felt him swell and redouble his efforts to fuck her senseless, she was desperate for some relief herself. The sperm, when it came, was thick and delicious as it spurted furiously into her and she had to swallow as fast as she could to keep up with it. Josef lifted her up as soon as he had tidied himself but she whimpered as he did so and he stopped, put her down and looked into her eyes.

"Alright!" he said, not unkindly. "Angel kill me if she sees me, but get your legs open!"

Eagerly she obeyed and felt his big, rough hand slide between her thighs, the coarse, hard skin of his fingers sending tingles right through her as it sandpapered over her clitoris before sliding into her molten hole, stretching its sides as he added a third finger to the two he had originally put in. He twisted them and she couldn't help making a soft yelp as she was stretched even further.

"Ssh! Stupid bitch!" he growled, but he slowed down his assault and in a few seconds was able to work four fingers inside her. Her legs trembled and her breath rasped as she tried to control the mounting crisis inside her but a moan bubbled out as he began to pump his hand up and down. Using his free hand he reached for her head and buried her face in his shirt to muffle her cries as he thrust, thrust, paused and then thrust again in response to her spasms. She let out a guttural growl as the orgasm drained from her and his hand was withdrawn. He let her get her breath back before hoisting her up once more and taking her back to her barracks.

"Stupid bitch!" he whispered cheerfully. "You get plenty fucking soon enough."

With her head banging gently against his back as he walked, Amelia happily accepted the truth of his remark. She felt relaxed and fulfilled in the post orgasm lethargy.

But most importantly, she was back where she belonged.

CHAPTER TEN

In the old days, as she thought of them, although it had only been about three years in reality, the arena stables had been small enough to display their stock in wonderfully erotic and inventive ways before an event. Amelia still remembered attending her first show at the Bakhtar arena and seeing the slaves in X shaped suspension so that their fitness and condition could be assessed by the crowds before bets were placed.

Their bodies had been beautifully decorated, some with armbands and necklaces of gold filigree, some with heavier bronze adornments pinned to their nipples and navels. On this occasion though, the host stable had clearly decided on a mass market approach. Amelia and her squad were herded into the long building she had seen the night before and put in two pens.

The pens were made of slender steel poles that stretched up to the roof but the pen itself was open to the elements. Only the terraced seating sloping up on both sides in two long banks and at either end was under cover. There were six of the pens, all well separated, standing in a row down the centre of the building. The CSL slaves and the Girl Squad's solo fighters were taken away and out of the far end of the building. Amelia thought they would be displayed somewhere else where the public could get close to them as their fewer numbers made it easier to display them intimately. For the squads there was only a press of about fifty of them in each pen. Once they were shut in, they saw the Orange squad being penned just along from them and for a few moments the two squads assessed each other, then gradually they relaxed and sat down on the bare, still-damp earth, lounging against the bars of the pens. However, some of the guards, equipped with cattle goads came round and in shrill angry voices urged them up, threatening them with the wicked prongs. Then the paying public was allowed in.

A multi-coloured and brilliant crowd surrounded the cages in seconds. Hands pawed at the girls through the bars and voices shouted at them in various languages and they shrank together into a huddled mass in the centre of the cage. But the guards forced their way through and gesturing with the cattle goads, urged the girls to spread out and allow the hands to grope them.

Amelia knew that this was standard practice at arenas and had been through it before but not quite on this scale of humiliation. But once she had decided she didn't want to try the cattle prods, standing by the bars with Seventy-six pressed close against her, had a masochistic thrill all its own.

The conversations beyond the bars seemed to be in every conceivable language apart from English, which rather emphasised the animal-like status of the English speaking slaves. The hands and arms that stretched through were not interested in any sexual groping, they were purely assessing muscle tone and amounts of fat carried. Amelia couldn't recall ever having her breasts mauled in such a remote and non sexual manner, but somehow that added to its thrill and before long the pen was richly scented with the arousal of the milling, naked slaves. It seemed to go on for hours before people drifted away and the squads were herded back to their stockades to wait for the opening parades.

The grooms and the female guards passed among them fussing and nervous as the early evening wore on and the girls sat on the edges of their cots and waited. Their hair was combed, their nipples were rouged. Amelia and Seventy-six were separated off and given special attention as they were entered in the dressage.

They wore eye make up and lip stick. Their cheeks had blusher brushed on. And then they were harnessed.

It was the decorative, dressage harness, the bridles had delicate silver work on them wherever the straps were wide enough, the blinkers were beautifully tooled and decorated, their girths had wide, oval panels at the fronts, across their stomachs and in a silver panel mounted on the leather was a picture of an arena slave with a whip. Around the edge Sadia's name and title were engraved with lavish decoration. Their cruppers had a row of silver studs running down the centre, drawing the eye to the way the straps spread their labia as they supported the dildos impaling them and then farther back kept the butt plugs firmly embedded. As the cruppers ran between their buttocks, they also supported a wire prong that rose up in a curve and in its turn mounted their tails, so that the hair would fall gracefully from higher up the buttock than if it had merely been hung from the plug.

For dressage it was vital that the tits didn't wobble and swing at different speeds and in different directions on each slave. Everything had to be choreographed to perfection and each stable adopted its own solution. Angel had decreed that each nipple was to be clamped with a small, polished silver, screw clamp. A slender, stainless steel bar ran between the clamps and chains ran up from each nipple to be clipped to the ring at the front of the high posture collar each slave wore. Thus a pleasing and decorative tri-angle was drawn on each girl's chest and her tits were steadied.

The groom who was tacking up Amelia and Seventy-six was an experienced woman who frequently played with them in the dungeons back home and often drove them. She took her time screwing the nipple clamps down onto the girls' excitedly erect nubs; gauging when she had got each girl gasping and wide-eyed to just the right degree. The last part was to feed the bits through their tongue rings and clip them to the reins and the bridles, then they were ready.

There was a sudden commotion as the stockade gates were flung open and the Girl Squad saw how they were to be paraded for the formal opening of the games.

With a silken black and yellow sheet, embroidered with complex swirling patterns and glittering with seed pearls, thrown across its broad back an elephant waited for them. Just behind its mahout sat Sadia in a howdah, resplendent in a gold satin full length dress and from the animal's flanks were draped many slender steel chains.

While Amelia and Seventy-six were harnessed to their trap and their driver settled herself, the guards began to clip the squad girls' wrists to the chains carried by the elephant.

Angel rode in a six slave racing chariot at the head of the procession, her blonde hair loose and blowing in a gentle evening breeze. Behind her came the dressage traps and behind them came the elephant leading a great fan of almost a hundred naked women behind it.

Slowly they made their way across the now-dry ground towards the floodlit bulk of the arena itself. Amelia's heart was thundering as they approached and heard the crowd. Already the home team had entered and there was wild cheering. Above the din the compere's amplified voice could just be heard and as they entered the darkness of the tunnel that led out onto the floor of the arena, Amelia just caught the words; 'Girl Squad!' being bellowed over the P.A.

Then they were out and momentarily blinded by the floodlights. The home team were just turning at the far end of the arena as the Girl Squad entered and from the edges of her blinkers Amelia saw masses of black and yellow and orange scarves being waved from the terraces. Paying careful attention to keeping in step with Seventy-six, they made their way around the arena and back into the tunnel and then back towards the stockade. But at the last minute they were steered to the right and with the three other dressage rigs, made their way to the clearing Amelia had seen the previous night, where there was a grass track and a level, mown infield. There they waited patiently while the crowd made its way over from the arena and the action began.

The final part of their preparation was to have their feet slipped into high-heeled ankle boots, which had been left off to minimise the risk of tripping during the parade.

Under the unreal brilliance of the lights and with the heat making their skins shine with sweat, the two teams performed their prescribed routines and their free-style ones devised by their trainers.

They backed their rig carefully between cones; turned it on a sixpence, traced curves and swerves on the grass in unison with other rigs as perfectly as they could, controlled by gentle taps with the carriage whip. They kept their necks arched and their plumes nodding as they gave a display of disciplined obedience that drew plenty of applause at its end. Then they stood, ankles tidily together at attention as the opposition performed. Inevitably the applause was greater for the home team but there was still the inspection. The judges came over and inspected the tightness of the girths and cruppers, looked at the polish on the studs and decorations, made sure the labia were parted as symmetrically as possible, ensured the tits were contained and controlled without any distortion of their shape. Female judges inspected their make up and grooming while the male judges stood back and Amelia heard them discussing the pertness of the buttocks and the shape of the thighs and how well, or not, the tits matched in each pair.

In the end the Orange team shaded the actual dressage display but the Girl Squad rig next to Amelia won best turned out rosette and she and Seventy-six got second. Each of them pranced and received a stinging lash across the buttocks as the rosettes were pinned directly onto the upper swells of their left tits. Then all the rigs paraded around the fence at the edge of the track and excited spectators leaned over and stroked them as they passed.

Then it was back to the stockade at a walk, and sleep as quickly as the grooms could strip them down. The next three days were going to be very crowded.

Tony took his seat in the owners' and trainers' box just in time to see the start of the first full day's first event. Eve was attending to the CSL stock held at the Girl Squad's quarters and they weren't needed just yet in any case. Angel and Amelia's strategy might prove disastrous, or very successful. It was going to be an interesting day. He nodded across cheerfully to Brian who was sitting on the other side of the box with Craig Maddox, the Orange team's trainer and their owner, a tall thin man with a greying moustache. He and Brian were honour bound not to contact each other in any way and had handed in their mobiles and notebooks as soon as they had arrived, but they exchanged tense smiles as they took their seats.

The P.A. crackled into life and the compere announced the twenty-a-side melee. There were cheers and as Tony looked around the audience and up at the big screens, he could see the expectant and excited faces, waiting for the action that would fuel the orgies to begin.

With a recorded blare of trumpets, the two teams marched out from the tunnel and into the brilliant sun. Each naked girl carried a small, lightweight shield and a heavy strap as her weapon. The straps were nearly a metre long and their blades tapered from almost six inches wide up by the ball handle, to a wicked point. The leather was heavy but very flexible. A strike with one made an excitingly loud noise but left comparatively little marking. However the clubbing impacts could drive a girl down fairly quickly and eventually raise some good weals but leave her able to fight again the next day. As the games went on though, so the weaponry became more testing.

Four judges came behind the two lines, they were appointed by the Owners' Council

and would signal when a girl had been down long enough to be counted out.

He checked the Orange line up and was not surprised to see Ayesha, Fiji, Ox and Trouble all lining up, pretty much as they had suspected. He had been in the dressing room where the slaves had been oiled and fitted up with their equipment, and he had watched as Angel had gone from girl to girl, running her riding crop across their breasts and explaining what they had to do. He just hoped that enough of them had been English speakers to understand.

Down on the sand of the arena floor the slaves had formed into two lines facing each other. The judges stood back and one of them fired a starting pistol. The two lines came together and the cameras greedily closed in on the shuddering breasts and parted thighs as the struggles began. The first overarm throws began to be exchanged and the smacks and cracks of leather on flesh were clearly audible above the cheering.

Almost immediately the CSL contingent went into its usual routine that had vanquished nearly all opposition in the past. Ox and Trouble worked as a pair, guarding each other's back, while Fiji and Ayesha worked close beside them, forcing their way through the enemy's line in a kind of phalanx and beating down any girl who stood against them.

Tony watched intently, ignoring the screens showing the first couplings and gropings on the terraces as the whips snapped at the naked flesh below. The Girl Squad fighters immediately in front of the CSL advance fell back and spread out, joining their sisters who were engaging Orange team fighters, several of whom now found themselves almost surrounded by enemies, all pounding them with their heavy straps. The CSL foursome had to split up to find opposition but every time they did, the Girl Squaddies faded away, preferring to bring down the Orange team first. And in little over a minute, one did go down, battered into submission by three of the Girl Squad. One of them stood over the fallen girl's head and dropped, her thighs spread wide, over the fallen girl's face. The girl didn't struggle and the cameras caught her tongue licking up into her conqueror's cunt. A judge blew his whistle and walked in to drag the fallen girl away, then the contest resumed. Once again the CSL contingent was frustrated and the Orange team members were hunted down. A blonde wearing the orange arm band was caught on the video screens surrounded by four of the Girl Squad. Her skin quivered as the straps hit her so fast she had no chance of fighting back, an uppercut from behind her doubled her over and her back took the full brunt of the whips until she went down.

And while that had been going on, the CSL slaves had been kept just busy enough, split up and scattered; kept away from the main action.

Tony smiled grimly as he recalled Amelia gesturing and pointing to get her message across that night on the veranda. But his loyalties were divided and he didn't glance across at Brian.

The cheering from the black and yellow supporters grew louder and louder. Another Orange girl went down. Two minutes later another two went down. Now the advantage began to tell ever more rapidly as the Orange team was increasingly outnumbered. The CSL contingent kept trying to bring their weight and strength to bear but the Girl Squaddies weren't having any of it yet, and retreated quite unashamedly rather than get drawn into a contest they couldn't win.

But when there were twice as many Girl Squad fighters as Orange ones left standing, the brakes came off and joyfully they flung themselves at their foes. However the foes were far from finished and Ayesha took a girl down with an elegantly devastating uppercut. Ox and Trouble battered another one to the ground but before the judges stopped the action to remove the fallen, two more of the Orange team bit the dirt as well.

The pause in the action was long enough for the conquerors to enjoy the fruits of conquest and so that the crowd could savour some salacious close-ups on the giant screens. Then it was back to business and there was no stopping until only the four CSL slaves were left, facing no fewer than twelve of the Girl Squad.

Tony suddenly realised he was gnawing his knuckles. Whichever team finally won the whole games, CSL would come out with credit – but he could see that things might never be the same at The Lodge if Amelia's and Angel's strategy worked. He glanced across at Brian and saw that he and Craig Maddox were already anxiously scanning the events ahead.

When combat resumed, the Girl Squad hunted in a pack and left just a couple of their number to fend off the remaining CSL slaves. They targeted Ox first and all the whip endurance training she had undergone at The Lodge couldn't help her. Five or six foes crowded round her and the spectators were treated to the sight of her skin rippling under the rapid salvos of lashes. Her big breasts swung and collided as lashes wrapped her from both sides simultaneously. Lashes curled up between her legs and wrapped her thighs lovingly but she simply didn't have time to fall. Desperately she swung her shield and lashed out herself but there was simply too much incoming for her to deal with.

Tony's eyes flicked up to the giant screens and took in the fact that on the terraces, women were being roasted and buggered everywhere. Others were on their knees, mouths full of cock, eyes swivelling sideways to miss nothing of Ox's thrashing, their hands busily working at their own crotches.

Down on the arena floor, Ox's arms dropped in exhaustion and she stood with her head bowed in the centre of a ring of foes who kept up the beating relentlessly. She dropped to her knees and still she was lashed, then she crashed forwards onto her face in the dust. Even then the excitement of victory led several of the Girl Squad to continue to ply the lashes until the judges pulled them off and dragged Ox away.

The compere addressed the crowds over the PA once the cheering had quietened sufficiently.

"Ladies and Gentlemen! I think we can safely assume the Girl Squad have won this event, don't you? I'm sure you don't want to see the last three girls suffer unnecessarily!"

The crowd gleefully joined in the pantomime and bellowed that, yes they did.

"But it can only be a matter of time now! I think we should call it off!"

The answering bellows nearly lifted the terrace roofing.

Of course the pause had only served to give the girls a chance to catch their breath, thus ensuring a longer and slower defeat.

Fiji was the next one targeted and like Ox, she was blitzed into submission. But not before she had flung away her shield and whip, and screaming defiance had flung herself bodily onto her tormentors. And while Ayesha and Trouble had been kept at bay, a furious wrestling match had taken place between her and three of the Girl Squad while whips had continued to lash the gleaming, dark skinned body, sending up sprays of sweat and oil into the bright morning air.

Trouble lasted no longer than her lover, Ox, and at last only Ayesha was still standing.

The arena was hushed. She had been almost as good as Blondie in her hayday but since leaving the Bakhtar stable had never really regained her form. Here she faced overwhelming odds. What would she do?

All round the world, arena aficionados leaned closer to their screens.

The whistle to resume combat sounded and she ran away. Black hair flying she streaked down the length of the arena floor. Behind her the squad leaped into action.

But then Ayesha stopped suddenly and turned, crouching she sent her whip scything out towards the leader of the pursuing girls, catching across the backs of both knees and brought her down in a cloud of dust. Then she was off again, running faster than her pursuers. Again she skidded to a halt and this time took out the lead pursuer with an uppercut that lifted the girl off her feet and made her twist like a hooked fish in the air before she crashed down. The crowd surged to its feet but now the Girl Squad spread out and began herding Ayesha towards the fence. And once they had her there, cornered, the crowd was treated once again to the sight of a beautiful body twisting, flinching and spraying sweat as it was whipped until finally a series of uppercuts dropped her to her knees and while her sisters finished the job, the girl who had landed the *coup de grace* lasciviously licked Ayesha's juice off her strap.

Then there was the punishment ritual. It was rare for the CSL slaves to find themselves at the mercy of the crowd and the crowd knew it too; and was dead set on making the most of the opportunity. A judge went to the centre of the arena and held up ten fingers. The crowd's thumbs came out pointing down. He snapped his palms closed and then open again, signalling twenty. The thumbs pointed down again. He snapped his palms closed twice, some thumbs pointed up but the compere decided it wasn't a majority. Only when forty had been signalled did the thumbs go up.

That evening, they would be treated to the sight of the losing team having forty lashes added to what they had already taken. Amelia and Angel had started the savage logic of the arena working in the Girl Squad's favour.

In the holding cells beneath the arena, Amelia listened to the cheering and wondered. The only clue she got was the cheerful demeanour of the guards as they came to take the solo fighters out to compete in the first of the duels. It would be with three tailed martinets today, the tails had been carefully weighted to add thud and snap to the square cut lashes. She prowled around her cell with her companions, listening to the noises above them and imagining the scenes being enacted. But it wasn't until almost the end of the first morning that she got to see daylight when they were taken out for the mass log pull.

As the slaves were piled into the dressing room and the grooms and guards rushed about oiling them till they shone, Amelia saw two of the solo fighters helped back in and Doctor Hooper start checking them over on the medical bench. She reckoned the Orange team had struck back. It wasn't unexpected and Angel didn't look too perturbed as she stood behind the vet and watched her treat the welts and bruises.

The door to the tunnel was thrown open suddenly and the whole squad crowded through into the twilight of the tunnel, already thronged with the Orange squad. There was much male cursing and snapping of whips as the girls were herded out into the blinding light and then guided towards their own telegraph pole sized log. Amelia stood quietly, waiting for her turn to have her wrists fastened to the heavy chain. On the terraces she knew that men and women would be manoeuvring towards a fancied partner for sex during the upcoming minutes. The mass log pull was a whip fest. Pure and simple. With two hundred naked female bodies, sweat and oil gleaming, toiling under the whips as their breasts swung and the lashes laced their backs, making their hair toss as they registered each impact. Some girls would grimace as they fought off the climaxes the flogging was driving them towards, others grimaced as they dealt with the pain in more cerebral ways, enjoying the humiliation even as they endured the pain for the pleasure of others.

"Lift!" The judge's voice cut through the air and the crowd subsided into watchful anticipation.

With crisp precision both squads hoisted their chains onto their shoulders and turned to face the front. Amelia, standing to the right of the log, settled the chain onto her left shoulder and leaned forwards as she took the strain. The girl in front of her was a striking Scandinavian blonde with a bottom that Amelia had loved kissing after a day under the whip. It would make for good viewing today as she would be close to it as it was flogged up, and then back down the length of the arena floor.

Each guard had five slaves to drive and Angel had drilled them into rhythmical accuracy in response to her commands as she perched on the log at the back and called the strokes. Amelia shook her hair back and glanced round to catch sight of her trainer, balanced and composed, standing on the log ready to drive her squad. She wore a short leather skirt and a leather waistcoat that strained across her breasts. Amelia caught her breath at the surge of lust she felt as watched Angel unfurl her whip.

The judge marched out in front of both teams, raised his pistol and fired it.

Instantly, in time to rhythmic shouts of; "Pull!" from Angel the whips began to fall. To start with, both lines, either side of the log planted their feet wide apart and swung the chain from side to side to 'break' the log from the dirt. They had been drilled into swinging left first and then right.

The rhythm of the calls accelerated as Angel felt the log begin to respond. The whips fell faster, the guards passing up and down their small sections of the line and lashing in exact time with the shouts. The slaves began to drive their paces forward more and felt the huge weight begin to stir.

Amelia only had the quivering globes of the buttocks and the straining thighs of the blonde ahead of her to look at as she hauled. But as the log moved so the girl leaned further forward and Amelia was given a view of the neat-lipped cunt she remembered fondly. It only made her wetter to think of the girl behind her having a similar view, and of course the crowd would be enjoying close ups on the video screens.

Meanwhile the whip stung her as it bit across her buttocks and shoulders, its thin leather tails leaving welts that the sweat ran into and stung. Before she had taken ten paces her hair was a matted tangle and sweat dripped from her nose. The broad hips of the girl ahead were already reddening and her buttocks were deliciously striped.

Another lash cracked across Amelia's upper back and she grinned as she felt her belly moisten even more. There would hardly be a female hole that wasn't being filled on the terraces right now. And later on, she would get her share. For now, she was just whipping flesh and loving it.

It seemed endless. Her chest burned, her legs felt they wouldn't support her and her breath hurt her throat. Even she was beyond any pleasure in the beating she was taking by the time the cry of; "Halt!" let them drop into the dust. And once it stopped, it felt so good! Her skin burned and stung deliciously. The sides of her breasts had taken several heavy thuds and throbbed excitingly and her thighs had also taken some well aimed encouragement in the final yards.

"You beautiful bitches!" Angel cried, striding along the log towards its front. "You lovely sluts! You won by two feet! Now take us home in style or I'll flay the lot of you first chance I get!"

Amelia exchanged wry smiles with the blonde next to her as they knelt up and waited for the drinks to come round.

The compere began calling out numbers and the lucky owners of those tickets began to scramble down the aisles to collect their prizes. While they were doing that the guards set about delivering what any well-flogged slave needs; a hard shaft of rampant cock.

As the Girl Squad had a fair few female guards, some of the less fortunate slaves had to content themselves with a mouthful of foraged –for cunt juice.

The lucky prize winners helped out with this chore by providing genitals for the slaves to caress and the crowd was entertained by mass blow jobs and cunnilingus. On this occasion, Amelia got a female member of the audience, her closest guard being sunk up to his balls in the generous mouth of the blonde next to her. The woman who presented herself in front of Amelia as she knelt on the sand was dishevelled, her hair tousled, her face flushed and triumphant and her T shirt was torn, revealing her left breast. Her short skirt was crumpled and her rather tubby thighs were streaked with sperm. She grabbed Amelia's hair with one hand and lifted her skirt with the other, spreading her legs as she did so. Amelia went to work willingly. She just wished she could see the screens and watch herself being humiliated. The girl yelled in jubilation as she briefly became the centre of attraction and the cameras found her, just as Amelia's tongue finally found its way through the wet, fleshy folds of the clit hood and lapped at the hardened little nub. It was a superb torment for Amelia, her hands were chained so there was no possibility of any relief for herself, but in between the plump thighs, the woman smelt and tasted so sweetly of depravity. As Amelia buried her head farther into the woman's crotch and licked up into the vagina, it drizzled a thick stream of fragrant juice laced with spunk onto her tongue. She had obviously been fucked repeatedly all morning and Amelia couldn't help wondering, as she used her ring to fetch groans of contentment from above her, how many cocks she had sucked to climax as well.

Eventually Amelia made the woman climax by grinding her ring and tongue against the woman's clit but she was thrown backwards contemptuously as the cunt finished spurting over her face.

At last there was water though, a bottle was passed along the row of kneeling slaves and although Amelia could have swilled the stickiness off her face as well as quenched her thirst, she chose not to.

The winning margin was a mere foot on the return run. And it went to the Girl Squad.

CHAPTER ELEVEN

As the sun set on the first day, Amelia and Seventy-six, gasping around their bits, their skins burning from the whip, muscles protesting, brought their rig home in third place in the two-in-hand race. Six rigs had competed on a roughly circular track that took them through shallow, muddy water, along tracks that ran between trees so tall and close that it was almost dark, across meadows of lush grass, through mud pools and finally brought them back to the well mown turf surrounding the arena complex. Every inch of the track had been lined with spectators as the girls had galloped under the lashes round five laps.

At one point, Amelia's rig had led but then Jet and Blondie herself had overhauled them. Even snatched glances from behind her blinkers made it clear to Amelia that the slaves were cruising and on the final circuit they had been passed by Sam and Legs. Amelia had been alarmed by their driver who seemed to be using the whip too much for this early in the competition. And where was the point in passing your own team? These thoughts went round and round Amelia's brain as her breath rasped and thundered in her ears as she pounded grimly for the line. It was only once she had been reined in that she remembered where she really was. The show was the thing! The driver of Legs and Sam's rig obviously knew they could take plenty of whip, so he gave it to them and put on a good show.

As they were led away to be hosed down and fed, Amelia heard the compere announce that the Girl Squad held a narrow lead as the single pony races got underway and she saw Purdy being lined up against Ayesha and Cherry being lined up next to an athletic looking blonde belonging to the Orange stable. There was no reason that the Girl Squad couldn't end the first day with their noses ahead.

Tony sat back and stretched until his joints cracked. He hadn't realised how tense he had been, but now the first day was over and he could relax. So far, so much better than they had dared to hope.

Angel joined him and Sadia in the owners' box and Sadia's hand immediately crept up the trainer's tanned thigh and slid under the leather skirt. Angel shifted her bottom and slid forward enough to allow penetration. Tony watched in amusement as her face softened.

While the races had been held, there had been more action in the arena; the two slave log pulling contests. The Orange team had had to field Ox and Trouble as one of their teams, despite the pounding they had taken earlier on. Once the team lists were handed to the judges at the start of the day, there was no changing allowed. The Girl Squad's teams of slaves had narrowly won in two of the pulls and lost the third. One of the wins had been over Ox and Trouble who now faced a further pounding at the whipping posts for losing. Tony doubted Brian would allow them to be entered for anything on the second day and even the third day was doubtful. Amelia and Angel's tactics looked to be working well.

As he watched Sadia's wrist flex as she rubbed her hand up and down Angel's slit, he realised that the beatings he had witnessed had left him with an erection that was urgently in need of attention. The arena was still filing up as people returned from the racing and took their seats for the punishment session. He left the owners' box and went in search of a spare female.

In the dressing room he found Eve was busy with hosing down exhausted competitors and leading them back to the holding cells before they were taken back to their stockade. Over by the treatment tables however, tethered by their tongue rings to the tack hooks on the wall were Amelia and her partner in the two-in-hand races. They were both facing the wall and Tony considered their back views before making a choice. Both sets of buttocks were deliciously marked, as were the upper thighs. Their backs were also liberally striped with the narrow pink lines typical of the driving whip. He approached them and stood beside them; they briefly turned their heads as far as they could and then went back to patiently staring straight ahead. He loved the way the arena slaves were trained to know that what was done to them was none of their business, they just waited until anyone wanted them. He compared their breasts; of course he was familiar with Amelia's tip-tilted nipples, Brian had frequently lent her to him at The Lodge. But Seventy-six's were altogether more sizeable and the nipples stuck out smartly to attention pointing straight ahead. He made his choice and ducked under Seventy-six's leash, unleashed Amelia and pushed her to her knees. Then he undid his trousers and manoeuvred his cock out, fed it into Amelia's waiting mouth and set about fondling the other girl's tits while Amelia ardently sucked on him, taking him down gently in ever deepening thrusts with her head. He closed his eyes the better to savour the feel of her mouth and throat, softly stroking every inch of his shaft. As he did so he gripped his hands in the softness of the brunette's tits. She groaned as his fingers clenched, Amelia ran her tongue teasingly across his meatus and Tony dug his fingers in deeper, aware that her driver's whip would have scored her breasts. Her nipples rubbed at his palms, erect and rubbery, enjoying their abuse.

Amelia dipped her head farther than before, taking him in deeper than ever. He twisted both the brunette's nipples and pulled them hard. She cried out around her tongue ring and he began to come. He felt the pulses running up his cock and Amelia felt him swell in her throat. She held her head steady and swallowed his emissions smoothly while he bucked his hips at her and mauled the other girl's tits even more harshly in his ecstasy. Then the storm was over all too soon and he tucked himself away once Amelia had cleaned him up. Then he tethered her again, smacked both girls on their rumps and let them get back to waiting for whatever was going to happen to them next.

Back in the arena the lights were on and out on the sand a varied array of frames and benches had been laid out. In batches of five at a time, the slaves were enjoying what the audience had wanted meted out for their having lost. The compere was calling seat numbers again and eager amateurs were joining in the fun. Some female audience members whose tickets had won them a chance to flog arena slaves were having trouble wielding the longer stock whips and were getting tutorials while the unfortunate slaves acted as targets for practice before their real beating could get underway.

Tony noticed that Ayesha, who had had to be almost carried in by a guard, having just lost in the single pony race was ankle suspended in a rectangular frame, her spectacular body was pulled into tension by ropes from her wrists. She was being seen to efficiently by a Girl Squad guard and several of the video screens had close ups of the way her gleaming olive skin flinched and quivered under the lash. Her superb buttocks in particular rippled perfectly. Her flagellator stopped and moved in as Tony watched.

"He's giving her a rest!" the compere crowed. And indeed the man took his time delving his hand deep in her cunt, swirling his fingers about. The crowd cheered as they saw her tethered and stretched body arch and wriggle as far as it could, then the hips began to rotate and buck. Even over all the noise of the other punishments, he heard her cry out. But then the man withdrew his hand and acknowledged the cheers as Ayesha went into paroxysms of frustration at being prevented from orgasming. The man wiped his fingers on her scored thighs and then went back to delivering the rest of her beating.

Ox and Trouble were hung by their wrists, back to back and the whip was applied to their fronts. After the pounding they had taken in the log pulling and the whip melee, even the two stalwarts of the CSL team were visibly drooping as their bodies swung like a pendulum while their breasts, stomachs and the fronts of their thighs suffered. Fiji was in the last group to be put to the posts and Tony reflected that there was something about the girl's aloofness that invited harsh punishment. They put her upside down on a Y shaped post, legs wrenched wide apart, facing outwards so the crowd could see her face. She took twenty on her breasts and belly and twenty between her legs. Despite remaining almost mute during the beating, she produced a visible spray of juice during the last few lashes of the cunt whipping.

Amelia snatched a couple of minutes' sleep after her evening meal and was then shaken awake by a guard and hauled up, tongue leashed and led out of the stockade. She knew she had been hired out and was heading for the playrooms that would be somewhere in the arena building.

As it turned out they were on the ground floor. And as she was led in on her leash, Amelia could see the room was well equipped to provide pleasure. There were already several slaves being enjoyed by dominants of both sexes. Apart from the guards who were delivering and removing the girls, everyone was naked and Amelia's eye was immediately drawn to the semi tumescent cocks, wagging between muscular male thighs. She was led past two men bending over a slave spread out on a rack. They were pegging her breasts which already had nipple clamps attached to a spreader bar above her. Her body heaved and arched as the pegs were added, muffled cries escaping from behind a ball gag. One of the men climbed on the rack and located his cock between her spread thighs...... but that was all she had time to see as she was tugged along and finally delivered to a couple; the woman was a tall, shapely brunette, the man was thick set with a rug of greying hair on his chest. They signed for her and the guard reminded them they had paid for an hour before leaving.

The woman was greatly taken with the tongue ring and leash and just led her about for a few minutes while the man selected implements to use on her. Some of the whips he chose looked very interesting and when the woman finally got round to feeling her, she was able to slip her fingers in with no problem at all.

They shackled her wrists to the arms of a wall-mounted X cross, with her back to it and the man beat her breasts and stomach with a wickedly stingy little flogger. Then they clamped her nipples and stretched the chains that the clamps were attached to up to a spreader bar above her. Then while the woman knelt and fellated him the man beat the undersides of her breasts. Amelia twisted and flinched under the stinging assault, her eyes watering, incoherent cries coming from her as the pain built and built and her ignored cunt ached for attention. She was about to scream in frustration when the beating stopped suddenly. She blinked her tears away and found the man had pushed the woman away and was lifting her legs to wrap around his waist. She co-operated eagerly and felt his fingers spread her lips as the broad shaft of his cock speared up into her. His woman knelt behind him and from the glazed look of delight that spread over his features as he fucked her, she guessed he was being rimmed as he fucked. He dug his fingers into her scorched buttocks as he came and she toppled over into the release of orgasm as well. After that the man took a back seat and let the woman loose on her. She put her face-up along the top of a bench and sat on her face while she used a suede tailed flogger between Amelia's spread thighs.

She tongued the woman to several orgasms and her mouth was awash with rich tasting cunt juice by the time the woman finally fell forwards and groaned her way through another orgasm. Then the man returned to the fray and simply climbed onto her and fucked her where she lay, wrung out and exhausted but still gamely trying to take him for a ride. Only him digging his fingers into her breasts revitalised her enough to bring her to a satisfactory climax.

It was several minutes before she was able to gasp and blink her way back to full consciousness and realise that her clients had gone. However Doc Hooper was standing over her, taking her pulse and checking her eyes with a guard beside her.

"She's fine for at least one more session," she decided briskly and turned away. The guard presented two men with a clipboard that they signed for her on and then he too left.

The men hauled her up and turned her round before putting her back on the bench face down. She took a roasting and felt aggrieved that in the wake of the orgasm that engulfed her as both men climaxed inside her, she might miss some of what was done to her.

And so it proved. The men contrived to keep one of them penetrating her while the other one beat her or tormented her breasts and nipples. She came until she was frightened of the intensity her climaxes were attaining and was only vaguely aware of being slung over a guard's shoulder to be taken back to her bed.

The second day of the games dawned as brightly as ever and the events got underway with combats in the pens and pursuit running in the arena. But before that, in the centre of the stockade, Amelia went through limbering up exercises with all the others, stiff and bruised, but eager for the day's thrills.

Tony helped with the final preparations in the dressing room, oiling the lithe bodies and checking that they hadn't gone lame overnight. Then he helped lead the chosen slaves out and tether them next to the horse corral. High boarding had been set up along the length of the arena and once the crowd who had chosen to attend this event rather than the pen contests, had settled, a judge took the first of the Orange team's competitors from their hitching rail and led her out to the starting line. He unclipped her leash, uncuffed her hands and fired his starting pistol in quick succession. The girl jumped and then quickly fled as she remembered what she was supposed to be doing.

The crowd cheered as her breasts swung and her buttocks rippled as she ran, desperately trying to stave off defeat for as long as possible.

The idea of Pursuit Running was simple. A naked girl was hunted down by a man on horseback from the opposing team. She was given half a lap's start before the horse was released and it was surprising how many laps a good runner could make, the arena was cramped for a horse and the sharp turns at each end of the boarding gave a girl a chance to prolong her run and improve her chances of pleasing the crowd enough to escape the punishment session at the end of the day.

Beside Tony the starting pistol fired again and the corral gate swung open. The horse, spurred on, pounded away just as the naked girl disappeared round the far turn.

The first run lasted for five laps before the rider curled his lash round the girl's thighs and brought her crashing down. He was off the horse in an instant and pinned the girl down. A further pistol shot signalled the end of that run and the rider took his reward.

It was entirely up to him whether he took her mouth, anus or vagina but while he was busy her fate was being decided by the crowd. The judge held out his hand with his thumb up and the crowd agreed. It was a sunny morning and five laps was not a bad start. She was spared the lash. The giant monitors showed her swallowing her conqueror's sperm as his thick shaft plunged in and out of her wide stretched mouth.

Then it was the turn of a Girl Squad slave.

Legs was first up and she made ten laps. It wasn't just her speed, it took the rider three goes to bring her down fully, she rolled, squirmed and wriggled each time she was brought down and managed to get to her feet before the rider could dismount. The crowd loved it and she too escaped the punishment session but her pursuer was angry at having been made to look foolish and she took several hard lashes from the long stock whip before she was fucked.

The next Orange team member made eleven laps but after her, Sam brought the house down as she sprinted for no less than fifteen before she was brought down in a cloud of dust and was taken from behind on all fours by the rider who took his belt to her back as he fucked her. It wasn't strictly within the rules but it amused the crowd so no one bothered to stop him.

The fourth slave to be released was on a hiding to nothing. The crowd hadn't sentenced one slave to a punishment yet and they surely wouldn't let this one off, no matter how well she ran. She made a respectable ten laps but the whim of the crowd sentenced her to forty lashes.

Purdy was next out and got an extra loud cheer as she set off, her big tits swinging heavily. But nevertheless she was fast and it took the pursuit rider several laps before he was even in with a chance of catching her with his whip. Then she began to duck and dodge in the way he and Brian had trained all the CSL stock. As soon as she heard the horse gaining on her she kept close to the centreboard and then darted out to try and startle the horse and make it check. She made that tactic work on several occasions and gained two extra laps before the horse caught up again. She dropped onto the sand of the arena floor, her long legs out in front of her in a skid that she had learned back at the stable and Tony applauded as the horse overshot her and was pulled up violently while she darted round it and was off on another lap before the rider could start off again.

She made seventeen laps and was brought down by her own exhaustion as much as by anything else. The pursuit rider treated her to a dozen or so heavy lashes from the stock whip as she lay gasping for breath before him, and he redeemed himself in the eyes of the crowd. The sight of her breasts quivering under the lash was well worth waiting for as far as they were concerned. He took her on her back, lifting her legs up onto his shoulders and really thrusting deep into her, the cameras following the thick rod of his cock as it disappeared into her and withdrew before plunging in again and the arena echoed to her cries as she was fucked by her eventual conqueror.

Next up was none other than Blondie.

Like Sam and Purdy before her, she was a product of CSL training and had competed in some of the earliest stagings of these events, and so had almost helped write the book on how a naked girl could avoid the lash for as long as possible.

She ran with all her customary grace, her long legs flying, her mane of hair streaming behind her. But her pursuer, a man who had joined Sadia's stable after half a lifetime in the saddle on the steppes, was older and more wily. He didn't bother trying to land the whip on her when she ran close to the centreboard and he didn't get so close the horse could be spooked. He knew Sam and Purdy had clocked good scores, so he had a bit of time to play with.

Tony had to admit that Angel had picked exactly the right rider to put up against Blondie. When he was ready to strike, he steered his mount out wide at full speed and curved back in to confront Blondie as she was about to swing around one end of the boarding and he brought her down in a clean, single lash that pinned her thighs together and wrapped her legs twice more to the shins. She went down backwards and was even dragged a few feet before the man sprang from the saddle and pinned her with an arm lock.

The crowd stood and applauded. It was one of the cleanest pursuits any of them had seen and even Tony was lost in admiration.

It wasn't until he was helping to lead the slaves back to the dressing room once the competition was over that he realised that it was the first time Blondie had ever failed to clock the most laps in a pursuit running event.

Sam's and Purdy's totals stood for the whole of the competition. Even Jet could only match Sam but not overtake her.

CHAPTER TWELVE

Amelia waited patiently to be led into the pens. The Girl Squad slaves were tongue tethered to hooks in the wall of a corridor which led out onto the long concourse that ran the length of the building. The steel barred pens stood in a row between banks of terraced seating. Angel had chosen her for a wrestling bout, beside her Seventy-six stood, kitted out in the leather corset and weighted fist straps of a boxer. Blackie was on her other side, naked like herself and ready for a wrestling bout, a few slaves along and Rose stood, kitted out for a boxing match too. This was where they would see if the strategy they had mapped out on the veranda would really pay off. If they could just hold their own in the arena then in the pens they could really hurt the opposition.

Just before a guard came to unhook her leash and lead Amelia out, Angel appeared, flushed and smiling, running her trade mark riding crop across her slaves' breasts.

"Give 'em hell in there, you bitches!" she said. "We've beaten them in pursuit running!"

Amelia's heart raced. Again that was better than they had dared hope for.

She was pushed into her pen at the same time as a brunette was pushed in through a door opposite and both doors were bolted shut. From the pens, there was no exit while both girls stood. In front of them and behind them the crowd stamped and cheered as both girls went into a defensive crouch and began to circle each other, looking for weaknesses.

Angel could scarcely believe what was happening. She strode up and down outside the pens, slapping her thigh with her crop in her excitement. To one side and behind a flimsy fence the crowd was getting into the spirit of the catfights taking place for their entertainment.

Most of the women in the audience were being given vigorous seeings-to from behind and although there were more and more of them attending the arenas these days, there were still plenty of men to go around, and most women had a queue waiting to take their turn. Some dominants had come equipped and as the squeals and grunts from within the pens became louder, so they were pegging the nipples and labia of their naked subs who knelt in front of them.

That little slut – Ninety-seven – had been right. If the squad could hold its own in the arena, then it could forge ahead going into the last day. And they had done more than that! They were in the lead mid-way through the day.

As she strode past a pen she paused as two naked bodies crashed into the bars and then recoiled in a spitting, hair pulling, tangle. Despite the grimace, she recognised Ninety-seven and smiled as she watched the girl grab at her opponent's crotch, lift her and throw her face first against the bars. She got an arm up to protect herself but Ninety-seven was right behind her and went in for a crotch hold. From behind she rammed her thumb into the girl's anus and her fingers into the vagina. With her other hand she got a fistful of hair and then lifted the girl off her feet, her whole weight resting on the hand in her entrances. It was a real crowd pleaser and Ninety-seven milked it, holding the wriggling, screeching girl aloft as long as she could before wrenching her hand free and letting her drop. With a despairing wail the girl folded into a foetal position, nursing her genitals, rolling on the ground.

Angel paused long enough to watch Ninety-seven stroll round the pen taking the applause and waiting until her opponent was ready to continue – there was no point in hurrying a good defeat.

As soon as the brunette staggered upright, Ninety-seven darted behind her, twisted her arm so the girl had to bend forward and then stood astride her head. Simultaneously she used her thighs to make a painful headlock and her free hand to start spanking her opponent's bottom. Angel felt she didn't need to watch any more, Amelia – or whatever the slut's name was, seemed well in command. Further along the line of pens Rose was putting the finishing touches to another wrestling bout, her foe was almost totally limp and needed to be supported between throws but the audience near her pen were loving it. As Angel passed, the CSL girl had her opponent by the hair and was teasing her, slapping her face and breasts, making her paw ineffectually at her tormenting hand, then she let go of her hair and before she could fall the CSL girl had a crotch hold engaged and was looking round at the audience as though asking whether she should hoist the girl. The girl herself was begging for mercy but the thumbs all came out pointing downwards. Rose gathered herself and lifted.

With the shriek still ringing in her ears, Angel moved on to watch Cherry coping easily with a boxing bout. And in the next pen, Seventy-six was locked in a struggle with her opponent. The two girls were leaning against each other, swinging their weighted fists at each other, trying to hit the parts where the tines on the insides of the leather corsets would dig in but in fact all they were doing was pushing each other's breasts onto the metal studs while their fists only hit their sides. But as Angel watched the Girl Squaddy managed to push her opponent away long enough to land a blow to her breasts and another to her stomach. The girl doubled over and turned away from her tormentor who calmly stalked her round the pen, picking her off at will.

Angel felt that everything was well under control and strolled back towards the dressing room beneath the arena in high good humour and ready for a lunch break.

The first event on the afternoon's agenda was a sixty-a-side melee with rather heavier lashes than had been used on the first day. With so many girls out on the floor of the arena it had not been thought possible to influence the result by very much. What was going to happen, would. In the end the Girl Squad fielded Sam, Cherry and Lucky from CSL and played their own reliable all rounders.

The rules were simplicity itself; a shot signified the start and the clock would run for an hour. At the end of that time, the team with most members still standing was declared the winner.

Although all the girls were armed, pretty much anything went; kicking, punching, hair pulling – it was all good spectator sport. Duels formed and broke up and clumps of desperately struggling girls formed, writhing on the floor and always the cameras kept a voyeuristic eye on the thrashing limbs, quivering breasts and squeezing hands. The whips smacked home sending up sprays of sweat and oil from the naked, gleaming bodies and on the terraces the orgies resumed.

Amelia sat quietly in her cell and listened to the cheering and the shouts. She was on next and it was what she had chosen for herself; the studded whip duelling. With her eyes closed she ran through all the moves she had been taught by Angel plus all those she had seen Carlo and Brian teach the CSL slaves.

A sudden noise made her open her eyes and she saw Tony entering her cell.

"Just thought I'd tell you how things are going," he said. "We wiped the floor with them in the pens. Only Fiji and Beast did any good. And it's honours even after the melee. About thirty each side left standing. Cherry did a fantastic job, took out five or six, and Sam and Lucky were close behind her. CSL's got some rising stars alright and it looks like the Girl Squad might come through this okay!"

His tone was light but Amelia could see that there was concern on his face too. Back at CSL there would a post mortem and it would not go unremarked that the younger girls had outperformed the older ones.

"Purdy did a brilliant run in the pursuit," he went on. "Even Blondie couldn't beat her."

Their eyes met. They both knew the significance of that.

Amelia stood up and put her tongue out. Tony had her leash in his hand and she knew it was time for her to go out and face Blondie with a studded whip.

In the dressing room, together with the other slaves she had helped select for this event, she stood with her hands on her head while she was prepared. Again she was oiled so that her body would shine in the sun and the whips would send up a visually pleasing spray for the cameras. Then she was equipped with her armour.

Ever since the studded whips had been introduced in the early, piratical and unregulated days of the arenas, owners and trainers had struggled to find the best way of presenting this event to the crowds. Everyone enjoyed seeing the exciting marks the lashes left but even the best trained slaves were sometimes reluctant to commit fully to the fray with them. And owners likewise were often concerned about lasting damage to valuable stock. Various devices had been employed to force slaves to confront each other but eventually someone had stumbled across the fact that if a slave had some protection for herself, she would be much more aggressive towards her opponent. The armour also gave the owners comfort that their livestock wasn't being too badly damaged. The whips themselves had also developed into long, plain hide lashes with the slightly blunted studs concentrated into a widened area at the end of the lash, giving it the ability to land a clubbing blow and leave eye-pleasing welts without drawing blood for some considerable time.

Tony and the guards buckled on shin guards, helped her step into a leather thong that provided protection from an opponent's upper cut and then buckled on a wide leather belt that protected her stomach at the front and her kidneys behind. The final piece of protection was a steel helmet that had projecting cheek guards and a panel at the back of the neck that went down onto her back. Then she was given her whip and a small lightweight shield.

When all six slaves had been prepared they were led out into the tunnel and came face to face with the opposition. Checking their clipboards the guards positioned each slave opposite her opponent. Amelia watched the tall blonde figure take its place opposite her and stare at her calmly. If she had felt any surprise at seeing one of her erstwhile grooms appear in a squad, Blondie had obviously got over it after the pony races.

The compere announced the next event and to deafening cheers they were marched out in pairs. While the voice blared over the PA, describing the delights to come and explaining the rules – such as they were; it was a count up how many were standing at the end event – Amelia tested the ground under her bare feet, seeing how firm or soft it was. The rains had held off and it was iron hard – even a little slippery.

She glanced up at the sky and saw that although it was bright overhead, there were signs of clouds building in the distance behind the grandstand roofs.

She drew her attention back to the job in hand as a judge strode out and raised his starting pistol. She shook out her lash, settled her legs apart and faced Blondie, her shield at the ready.

Tony, Angel and Sadia all sat forward as one as the pistol was raised. In the owners' box there were video screens all down both sides as well as the best view in the house directly in front as it was situated over the entrance into the arena. They had played their three best solo fighters and added Amelia, Sam and Lucky for this event. The Orange team was playing Blondie, Tigre and the imperturbable Fiji along with the cream of their own stable.

The pistol fired and unlike with other events a watchful hush settled over the arena. Aficionados of the arenas would play and replay videos of these fights, discussing every lash and every dodge each girl employed.

If they could just draw this fight, the home team would have an uphill struggle on the final day. Tony chewed his knuckle distractedly as he watched Blondie step confidently forwards, swinging her lash in a lazy-looking overhead throw. Amelia ducked and covered with her shield and backed off.

The whip clattered harmlessly against it and Amelia flicked out sideways with her own lash. Blondie twisted and used her shield to guard her hip, then launched another strike; this time she crouched and swung low. Amelia leapt back and again caught the lash on her shield, then swung overarm and Blondie wasn't quite quick enough to sway backwards. The lash thudded home – audibly even in the terraces - on one shoulder. There was a gasp from every quarter as the famous blonde visibly flinched and then skipped back to regroup.

"Don't waste energy!" Beside him Angel was whispering through tensely gritted teeth. "Make her come to you, you lovely bitch!"

As he glanced sideways, Tony saw on one monitor a close up of Fiji already finishing off her opponent. The unfortunate brunette was reeling backwards trying desperately to delay the time when she would have to turn her back and take the full fury of the whip there. Inevitably she lost her footing as she backed and went down, sprawling in the dust. From there on it was just a matter of time. He turned back to the arena itself.

Amelia resisted the temptation to follow up her early success. She knew that Blondie would exploit any weakness she showed in coming forwards. Instead she kept just at the limits of Blondie's whip, making her come forward, making her expend energy. It was very rare that an opponent struck the first blow against the tall blonde and it rattled her out of her normal, calculating calm. To Amelia's delight she strode forward and tried to bludgeon her way through Amelia's defences but she found that if she kept her concentration and stayed alert, she could deflect the strikes quite easily. And she kept backing away.

Once, Blondie stopped pursuing and Amelia nipped in quickly. She used her shield to knock her opponent's whip out of the way and launched a bruising blow that wrapped Blondie's middle back and the studded head of the whip thudded home on the side of her right breast. She cried out and even through her adrenalin haze, Amelia heard the arena applaud. Two good, marking lashes without a reply from Blondie herself. It was unheard of. And now Blondie seemed to recognise the significance. She launched a blistering attack, swinging the lash fast overhead and then bringing it low, trying to bring Amelia down, but Amelia kept backing off and working her shield, dodging and skipping lightly on her feet.

After a few moments she saw what she was after. The attack faltered and Blondie stood before her, chest heaving and sweat running freely down between her breasts. It dripped off her nose and she had to wipe her forehead to clear her eyes. Amelia took a quick swipe and caught her across the fronts of her thighs, then skipped backwards.

Time had at last caught up with the great Blondie. Angel had seen it when she visited CSL and Amelia had noticed it too in her last days there. If she could make the big blonde work, after the pony races and the pursuit running, she could bring off a victory that would be the talk of the arenas for years to come. Whatsmore she could reduce the threat Blondie posed in the chariot racing on the final day.

Then the rain came.

There was no warning, no light drizzle first. Suddenly the naked girls were being pounded by drops of rain that felt like hailstones. Instantly they were blinded and sodden, their hair hung in rat tails, plastered over their faces. And beneath their feet the ground turned into a quagmire. The floodlights clicked on and the girls' bodies gleamed in the strange blend of stormlight and artificial light.

Blondie's experience saved her, Amelia later realised. For a fatal second she had looked around at the tableau around her. Girls downed and holding shields up desperately. Girls already defeated being dragged away; Fiji acknowledging the cheers. Suddenly Blondie's lash smacked across the width of her back, knocking the breath from her and jolting her forwards. She lost her footing and sprawled face first into the mud. Immediately, ignoring the pain of the lash as best she could, she twisted and caught the next lash on her shield, then tried to wriggle away. Blondie had to brush her hair out of her eyes and that allowed Amelia to get to her feet. Both girls charged and both fell as their feet slipped out from under them. They collided chest to chest on their knees and struck out wildly with their shields and the handles of their whips. Amelia fell backwards with the bigger girl on top of her and they rolled and wrestled in the mud.

It was just as Amelia had feared. The arena was one huge mud wrestling ring now and there was no room for any science or tactics. It was just a case of lashing out with fists and feet and hoping. But steadily Blondie's weight and strength told until she was sitting astride Amelia's chest. Her skin and hair were a rich grey-brown colour; the colour of the mud around them that shone in the harsh light and while Amelia clawed desperately at her breasts, Blondie managed to deliver a blow with the handle of her whip that left Amelia dazed and immobile.

In the owners' box Tony and Angel were trying to identify which shining mud sculptures were Girl Squad and which were the Orange team. But one camera caught Blondie's features as she staggered upright and they could both see the weariness there and the way she was gasping for breath.

"If it hadn't rained, that little bitch would've had her!" Angel cried. Tony couldn't disagree.

CHAPTER THIRTEEN

Amelia was given a check up by the vet once she was back in the dressing room and pronounced perfectly fit, apart from a heavily bruised cheek.

"Still whoever wants you tonight isn't going to be taking you to the opera!" she said cheerfully. "So you'll do for where they will be taking you." And she tweaked a nipple playfully before moving off to attend to a badly sprained ankle on the slave beside her.

The rain had stopped as suddenly as it had begun and from what Amelia could make out, Sam and Lucky had prevailed in their contests but the Orange team had scraped home. But that left the teams almost neck and neck for the final day, the Girl Squad had a slight lead but if they put a foot wrong, they would lose. As she lay on the bench, from which no one had bothered to free her, she heard all the talk, which was about how close she had come to defeating Blondie.

She was torn between a feeling of sadness for Brian and Carlo and elation at the thought that hers and Angel's strategy had worked.

Once again she managed some sleep after the evening meal before she was woken and taken to the playrooms. To her delight the first couple who had booked her wanted medical play and put her on a bench which had stirrups for her calves and feet. It represented a welcome change to the more customary floggings she was subjected to. They strapped her in, then raised and spread her legs but left her hands free, so she was able to prop herself up and see what they were doing. The woman laid a clean white towel across her lower stomach while the man laid out a clanking row of shiny steel appliances just beyond her spread-open crotch. On the towel the woman laid out sterilised packets containing needles. Above her knees hung a spreader bar.

The spreading, clamping, piercing and weighting went on for an hour and Amelia loved every minute of it, especially when they introduced a dilator and opened her wide. She was ecstatic at being so minutely examined, with her labia pinned back and clamped open, vulnerable and delicate as a butterfly, while the shiny, cold, hard machine was pushed into her and then remorselessly opened in front of both of them. When she was as wide open as she could be, they set about her clitoris, piercing the hood and then setting her off on the climb to orgasm by just pricking the throbbing nub itself. The woman beat her across the breasts to encourage her climax and when it came, the man watched closely and his presence seemed to spur her body on. When she came she felt the hot wetness spurt down her cunt and she produced a real squirt of juice, something she hadn't done since a particularly good session back at the stable, some weeks previously. It was almost a disappointment when the man released some of the chains and clamps he had used on her lips and simply fucked her before instructing the woman to remove the needles.

The next people who had booked her were a group of three men who had clearly clubbed together to afford her and made full use of her for an hour and a half. They seemed very keen to explore her anally and by the time they had finished, she was walking very stiffly and awkwardly. But at least those parts of her that the arena had taken its greatest toll of had not been too badly dealt with and she fell asleep, quietly proud of being the girl who had almost beaten Blondie.

For some enthusiasts the six slave chariot racing was the real focus of the games. The action was fast and furious and form was assiduously studied between events. Amelia had always enjoyed watching them when she had been a free woman and was proud that she and Seventy-six provided the main push for one of Sadia's rigs, they were shackled to a cross bar directly in front of the lightweight, two man chariot. The driver would wield the whip across their backs. In front of them was a wider cross bar with four slaves shackled to it. The middle two, like Amelia and Seventy-six had both hands on the bar, but at either end of the bar the slaves only had their inner hand shackled. Their other forearm was armoured in a mail sleeve to be used in battle against other teams, usually at the turns. The whipman, equipped with a long driving whip of weighted whipcord, would ensure all four were kept on their toes. He would also wield it against opposition slaves. Thus the outrunners at the front took the brunt of the whip play.

On this particular day though, all eyes were on the Orange team. Ayesha had taken a pounding on day one and Blondie had almost come unstuck on day two. Both slaves were renowned for their abilities as front outrunners and fighters.

Amelia smiled grimly to herself as she waited for the finishing touches to be put to her harness in the circus. Both the famous slaves were present, although she'd have been prepared to bet that Brian had got precious little sleep the previous night.

But she didn't have much time to worry about the Orange team because Angel came to finish off their tacking up, and the camera crews followed closely.

She was carrying the steel bowl that was known and feared by all the chariot racing slaves. Every trainer had one; it was their unique blend of spices that would be used to coat the anal prong inserted into each slave to make her concentrate on reaching the finishing post just as fast as she could. It was at least as effective as the whips and the cameras loved the close ups.

Angel approached from in front of Amelia's rig so Amelia could see her trainer from between her blinkers as she and a guard began to make the front rank bend over and accept the torment. The thick gooey mixture was dolloped onto the prong which hung from the crupper strap that had been left dangling between each slave's legs. Then the dildo was slipped into the vagina, enabling the anal plug to be located between the bent-forwards girl's buttocks at the anal opening. Angel took a firm hold of the crupper with one hand, steadied the nose of the plug and then pushed and pulled simultaneously. Inevitably there would be a bit-muffled squeal as the steel was suctioned in and the sphincters were spread wider and wider until the flange at the base was safely lodged tight against the opening. The cameras followed the intrusion into girl after girl and the audience never seemed to tire of the sight of the steel sinking in and the slave's grimace as she was first penetrated and after few moments more, began to register the stinging inside her.

To add to the fun, both owners had agreed to studded tack and even the crupper that ran down the belly and back up between the buttocks, before being buckled tight to the girth, was studded.

However much Amelia liked the idea of being so shamelessly spread for the amusement of the crowd, the previous night's use and Angel's devilish elixir made her eyes water and she was shaking her head and prancing as prettily as the next girl by the time they were lined up for the first race.

Throughout the morning they raced in pairs; there were three rigs from each team and points were accumulated as each pair raced all the opposing ones with a rest in between each race.

After each race the cruppers were unbuckled and for a moment the girls could relax, a guard usually pushed a damp sponge up into their rectums to clean them out before the next dose was administered. The double plugging and the stud that rasped infernally against her clit together with the pain from the brew inside her and the whip on her back, made Amelia weak kneed with arousal and excitement. Thankfully two of the female guards, after their second race, came round and administered a brisk rub to each throbbing clitoris so that a manageable orgasm was attained and the final race was fought out by slaves concentrating properly on the job in hand.

Amelia's driver was the one she and the rest of her crew had got used to in training and although one of their usual outrunners had been replaced by Lucky – Amelia's suggestion – the rig performed well, winning two of its races.

In the final race of the morning all six rigs took to the track at one time and there were double points at stake, so that a team which was ahead after the paired races could still be overhauled in the final. It made for excellent viewing as the slaves were tiring and the whips had to be used hard, and in addition with so much at stake there was no quarter given at the turns and in overtaking manoeuvres. Anything a driver or whipman could do to bring down the opposition, they could be relied upon to do.

As Amelia's crupper was pulled up hard for the last time and her abused perineum and rectum absorbed yet another dose of pain, her watering eyes made out her own bottom up on one of the giant monitors. A miniature camera had been placed on the front of the chariot, just behind her.

The compere came on the PA to confirm that the audience would be 'riding with' no fewer than three of the rigs, with cameras right in the thick of the action at the front crossbar and with a beautiful view of the buttocks the driver was whipping, from the cameras on the chariots themselves.

She had no idea of the overall score as her rig took its place, drawn in the middle for the start of the final race. All she could do was draw in her breath and gather herself for one final effort as the judge paced out some way down the arena floor and held up the starting pistol.

As soon as it sounded the whips fell and the drivers yelled. Amelia pistoned her tired legs once more and tried to lose herself in the various pains that beset her – making the delicious thuds of the lash on her back and bottom mask the tiredness. At the first turn the battle up front was fierce, Lucky's back was wrapped by an expert lash from another rig's whipman. She reared and twisted but still managed to elbow off a challenge from Ayesha, allowing her rig to corner well enough to challenge the rig inside it on the next straight. Just before the second turn they caught it and their driver performed a perfect door-slamming move. He wrenched his reins hard right, dragging the front row of slaves' heads round and steering the chariot towards the centreboarding. The opposition's rig had nowhere to go and slammed into the Girl Squad chariot itself. Orange team girls were thrown into the air as they tripped and the rig turned over at full speed. The driver was flung forward and landed just beside Amelia's feet, rolling swiftly and curling up to try and avoid the flashing feet of the racing slaves all around him. Briefly she caught a glimpse of Ayesha, trapped by her one shackled wrist, thrown down just behind him as the end of the front shaft suddenly dug into the sand and catapulted the slaves forwards.

Amelia had no way of knowing whether it brought down any other team until the next lap when she glimpsed two wrecks pulled out of the way and their teams being led out. One of them was a Girl Squad chariot with Legs and Blackie running in its crew.

With only four rigs left the cornering was not quite so crowded and the race began to settle down to one of sheer speed. And that meant lashing the last ounce of strength out of the slaves. The driver now kept up a constant rhythm of lashes in a relentless figure of eight pattern, so that when Amelia wasn't getting the lash, Seventy-six was. And overhead the long driving whip sang and snapped. When the sweat that was now pouring from her allowed her to see anything at all, she could see the backs of the front four girls were now almost ablaze with colour as the whipman expertly wrapped them and sometimes struck with the weighted tip directly.

She had no idea how many laps they had covered nor how many were left, her legs had gone numb and pumped mindlessly, her breath came in great sobbing gasps from her raw and burning throat. And around the bit that passed through her tongue ring, saliva flew from her helplessly open mouth and helped cool her throbbing breasts. And all the time the whip fell and her backside burned horribly.

Then suddenly the rhythm of the whip changed. From somewhere the driver summoned up more strength and began really laying into his part of the team. Automatically Amelia responded to the change without realising that she had any reserves left. For a few hectic minutes and one corner where they were wrenched around mercilessly without slowing in the slightest, Amelia strained like she had never strained before and then her head was being wrenched back and the whip had stopped. Her legs went from under her and she collapsed, Seventy-six landed, gasping, on top of her and then, after a few moments of heavenly relief, she felt the driver reach down and begin to unbuckle the hated crupper strap.

She opened her eyes and groaned as best she could as the prong was eased free of her bottom and the stinging began to recede, up on the screens they were replaying the last corner of the race and she could see from the front camera on her rig that they had been locked wheel to wheel with the leading Orange chariot. As she watched she saw Lucky striking out at Jet even as both slaves got the full benefit of the opposing driver's wrath. The two rigs had stayed locked together down the frantic last straight and the camera blurred and shook as the chariot hurtled the last few yards, the smacks of the whips and the gasps of the slaves all clearly audible and then the line had been crossed and as the drivers reined in the camera recorded the collapse of the slaves onto the ground.

"Results of the chariot racing are as follows!" boomed the cheerful voice of the compere. "Orange team thirty-six! Girl Squad, thirty-four! That means that in the final melee, the Orange team must score at least sixty points to win!"

Amelia's breathing began to ease as Tony and Angel strolled past.

"Pretty good," Tony was saying. "Second by a whisker and third too! If we'd won one more of the pairs we'd be home and dry now."

Angel flexed her crop thoughtfully. "Still, Ayesha, Blondie and Jet have been slowed down pretty well, so I reckon we're still going into the finale with our noses in front."

She looked down at the tangled heap of naked bodies still in their traces. "Come on!" she yelled at her staff. "Get these lazy bitches up and showered off! They've got work to do still!"

After only a light lunch of cold meat and salad, with a short nap after it, the two squads found themselves back in their dressing rooms being prepared for the final event. With all hundred girls present plus the CSL contingent, it was a chaotic scene as the naked bodies were once more oiled and all cuffs and collars removed again. Then in a jostling, excited herd of girlflesh they were driven out into the blinding light of the arena to see what awaited them.

Once Amelia's eyes had adjusted to the glare she saw that the floor of the arena had been partially fenced off, or rather fencing had been used to alter its shape. Instead of the oval it normally was, it was now an hourglass shape, with small-mesh, plastic fencing mounted on stout poles, curving in from both sides of the arena to make a narrow corridor about half way along. The corridor ran for about twenty feet and then the fencing widened out again. And in the far area there lay piles of whips, nets, quarterstaffs and behind them an array of whipping posts of various designs.

"…..once they do manage to get through the corridor," the compere was saying, "then the fun starts. Obviously if more of one team gets through before the other, they'll have an advantage. And they'll have the weapons to give us some really excellent sport! Remember, if the Girl Squad bring down forty-one of the Orange team, they win. If the Orange team can bring down sixty; they win. Either way, once that threshold's been passed, we can get down to the *real* business of the day!"

Amelia felt a warm tide of excitement spread through her belly at his words. Next to her a fellow slave shifted excitedly and the two exchanged grins. A siren would sound as soon as one side or the other had won and then the guards from both stables would be let loose plus a horde of onlookers whose ticket numbers matched those the compere was now calling out. The battered, exhausted girls would then face men – and some women – who were fresh and keen to enjoy a victory in an arena. The resulting struggles could only end one way. The floor of an arena after a final was a grand orgy.

Away on the Girl Squad's right, the Orange team were tensed and ready, Amelia saw Ayesha, Jet, Blondie and Tigre, all crouching as a judge strode out and raised his pistol.

There was the familiar dry, Crack! and they were off.

Two hundred girls threw themselves at a corridor no more than ten feet wide. At once Amelia found herself in the vanguard, running alongside Purdy, Sam and Lucky with four of the Girl Squad's best fighters grimly keeping pace, Legs and Rose were close behind. She glanced across and saw Jet pulling clear with three other squad fighters, Blondie was close behind but Ayesha was failing quickly, favouring one leg – maybe a strain picked up in the racing. But then there was no time for thought. The two groups arrived at the opening to the corridor simultaneously and behind them came the main weight of the squads. Amelia found herself locked in combat with Jet, her gleaming ebony body warm and slippery against hers as the press became worse and worse as more and more girls threw themselves into the fray. Jet's forearm caught Amelia under the chin and she was thrown against the fence face first, finding herself staring at a grinning cameraman filming her from just a foot beyond the fence. Jet pressed her harder against the plastic and Amelia couldn't move – but she could see her own face on a monitor and watched herself cry out as, from behind her, she felt Jet's hand ram between her legs and her thumb spear up into her anus while her fingers slipped into her wet cunt. Then the arena and the sky were pinwheeling horribly as she was lifted up and Jet's fingers gripped the septum between her entrances. Her hair was wrenched painfully and she felt herself thrown bodily through the air. Her training took over even as she registered the pain inside her as Jet's fingers gripped and then slid out of her, she rolled as she hit the ground, then gripped her abused parts and rolled some more. The stinging wasn't too bad but it always paid to put on a show, and in any case it was a welcome chance to rub at her clit for a few seconds. It wasn't often she had the use of her hands.

When she felt it was advisable and her frotting had overcome any discomfort from the throw, Amelia scrambled up and rejoined the struggle. The corridor was a mass of struggling, naked girlflesh and the cameras were having a field day. Some of the fights involved four or five combatants. And there were an increasing number of girls who were already down and who were now trying to claw their way back up or bring more down. As she watched, somewhere at the far end of the corridor, someone must have fallen and it caused a domino-like collapse of the maul. Legs waving and hands clutching helplessly the naked scrum collapsed and Amelia saw her chance to join in the battle proper. She took a run up and launched herself through the air, landing on soft female flesh – which squealed. Then with a wriggle and a somersault she was through.

Without wasting a second she ran forwards and picked up a whip, but no sooner had she got a grip on its rubber, cock-shaped handle than she took a heavy blow between her shoulders and went down again. This time it was Tigre, who somehow had slipped through the scrum, bruised and welted from the first day and from the racing but still swinging a whip for her owners. She loomed over Amelia as she sprawled on her back, the lashes of her whip black against the bright sky behind her as she brought it forward and down. Amelia rolled onto her stomach and kicked back and up as hard as she could, the whip landed hard on her middle back but she felt her feet make contact with something soft. She leapt up and saw Tigre winded and writhing on the ground and hoped that a judge would spot her and mark her as a point for the Girl Squad, even if she did get up again eventually.

She grabbed her whip and went to the aid of Seventy-six who was being held by one girl from behind while another belaboured her lovely tits. Amelia wasn't having that and took out the whip-wielding girl with one well aimed uppercut. Seventy-six threw the girl who had been holding her and dropped on her, digging her elbow into her stomach. Neither girl seemed to be in a hurry to get up and Amelia was immediately attacked by two more Orange team girls. One came in low and took her legs, the other landed on top of her as she fell backwards. There was a moment of almost pleasurable contact, breast to breast and crotch to crotch but then the girl scrambled off and held her arms fast above her head. The girl who had tripped her now squatted on Amelia's knees and began to lash her breasts and stomach. But the redheaded Sam toppled backwards over her, locked in a struggle with a squad girl, before she could get off more than a dozen or so lashes and Amelia wriggled free and leapt up. She saw the Orange team girl's arm raised to deliver a finishing blow to Sam who was pinned under her and she caught her fist, twisting her arm high up behind her back. The girl screamed and toppled forwards. Sam wriggled out from under her and while Amelia held her down, Sam laid into her backside with her whip.

Suddenly the wail of the siren went up, rising to a deafening crescendo that stopped all the girls in their tracks.

"Girl Squad win!" the compere bellowed.

Panting and laughing, Amelia stood up and looked around at the dust-covered, battered and bruised girls climbing slowly to their feet. Veterans among them knew that whatever had gone on before, it was every girl for herself now. Her only job was to entertain the crowds by giving as good an account of herself as she could before going down to inevitable defeat and use, right out in the open on the arena floor while the cameras recorded and replayed every detail of every humiliation.

Pouring through the now-empty corridor came all the men and a smattering of women with strap-ons. All were naked and all were armed with heavy tailed floggers. Some of the men sported exciting strapping and rings on their erect and wagging cocks

Amelia smiled at Sam and the Orange squaddie. Then as one they uttered a wordless scream and charged.

The first man Amelia took on, simply picked her up and threw her down onto her back in a thrillingly easy move, and before she could start to rise, he was lying on her, his hand was between her legs and she felt his broad helm push easily into her. For the sake of it she struggled a little but knew that really her job was to take as many as possible for a good ride. She braced her feet in the dust and thrust her hips back at him as he plunged into her and he smiled down at her before levering his torso up enough to allow him to duck his head and take a nipple into his mouth. Amelia cried out in pleasure as he nipped and suckled, his hard shaft ploughing her insides to a boiling cloud of exquisite sensations. She abandoned herself, flinging her arms above her head and giving herself utterly. She just hoped a camera was on her.

When he had spilled himself and gone on to the next, she sat up and then climbed wearily to her feet. Everywhere girls were either looking for their next conqueror or were surrendering to the current one.

Amelia limped towards a whip and picked it up, feeling the sperm begin to ooze down her thighs. A man strode towards her, she thought it was one of the Orange team's guards and she swung the whip in as strong an overarm throw as she could muster. He simply twisted and caught her wrist from below, then swung it back and up behind her. The whip dropped and she was bent forwards, crying from the pain until she dropped to her knees and then bent her head until her cheek was rubbing in the dust of the arena floor. She knew where this was leading and sure enough she felt his hand use the sperm she was leaking to lubricate her sore anus and as she opened her mouth wide in the expectation of pain, he steadily pushed himself up into her rectum, spreading her cruelly wide. She yelled, knowing he would like that but helpless to do otherwise. He paused and then thrust again, again she yelled. He paused once more and she opened her eyes wide as she gulped in air. There, up on a giant monitor and spurring on the crowds to their own acts of abandoned licentiousness, was her face, grimacing and crying as the man behind her took her. He thrust one more time for full penetration and she watched her mouth open wide as her passage was opened almost equally as wide and behind her the man took his pleasure with her. She collapsed in an ecstatic heap when he left her and it was some time before she could totter upright once more to see what more punishment she could find.

Legs spread wide to keep her balance, covered in dust and sperm, she staggered towards another whip, but strong male hands grabbed her by an arm and spun her round, she dropped dizzily to her knees, which was where he wanted her. And she had no strength to oppose his demanding hand in her hair, guiding her face onto his rampant, glistening cock which only just fitted her gaping mouth and which spurted its jism hard enough to make her choke.

She fell forwards onto all fours when he pulled free of her and wiped himself in her hair. She took a few minutes to get her breath back before she once more struggled upright. She wanted Sadia to be proud of her and wanted the crowd to remember how tough the Girl Squad had been to put down. And, she smiled to herself, just how much cock they could take!

All round her various struggles were taking place. The number of girls still able to stand was getting smaller so the ones who were able to were getting more attention. Amelia went to the aid of a girl – unrecognisable under the mask of dirt and sweat and sperm drenched hair, who was being held from behind by one man, his arms pinning hers, while a second man was flicking her across the breasts with a whip and giving her uppercuts between the legs whenever her struggles gave him the opportunity. Amelia charged joyfully into the whipman, grabbing him by his muscular thighs and trying to bear him down as she would a girl fighter. It didn't work and she found herself picked, upside down.

"You carry on with that one," he called to his companion. "I'll deal with this one!"

He let her fall and then dropped on top of her. Even as the breath was forced from her by his weight, Amelia was overcome with the pleasure of having a male body on her again. Her hands roved over the muscles of his back and delved lower to savour the hardness of his buttocks, so unlike the yielding softness of the female ones she was used to. He was all business and without glancing at her, even as he lay on her, he moved himself up her until she could feel him begin to slip inside her without even a guiding hand being necessary. She spread her legs wide and drew her thighs up to widen herself and felt him piston into her until she was stuffed to the neck. She nuzzled and kissed his hairy chest as he plundered her innards, jerking her violently about as he reached his climax and rammed himself hard into her. She came and came again, so powerfully that she hardly noticed his leaving and lay there, gasping and wheezing her way back to consciousness.

Beside her, the girl she had gone to help stirred and sat up, smiled down at her and lurched uncertainly to her feet. Amelia could see the gleaming trails of sperm leaking from her bottom as she staggered away. It had been Rose.

Grimly determined not to be outdone, Amelia got herself up and found a woman coming at her with a huge strap-on wagging from her waist as she trotted forwards, heavy breasts lurching and swaying on her chest. She launched a clumsy swipe with her whip as she approached Amelia and although normally she would have dodged it easily, exhaustion made her lose her balance and fall backwards onto something soft and slippery. She twisted round and found she had fallen onto Purdy's breasts. The CSL slave was lying on her back and as Amelia turned over she saw that the breasts, heaving most attractively and beautifully whip-striped had been wanked over. Purdy lifted her head and smiled at her as the woman with the strap-on knelt behind Amelia, who dipped her head and began to lap the fluid from Purdy's soft curves. She grunted as the huge plastic invader sank into her and knew that this could be the end of her afternoon. Women with strap-ons could outlast men and drain the last resistance from the most determined of slaves. But afterwards, Amelia had to admit that it was a good way to go. The taste of the sperm licked from Purdy's sweat-streaked breasts had been divine and the woman had encouraged them to further intercourse as she had fucked Amelia into a twilight world of almost constant orgasm. They had kissed and Purdy had sucked at Amelia's nipples, then the woman had withdrawn long enough to turn Amelia so that she could bugger her over Purdy's face while an ecstatic Amelia lay face down between Purdy's spread thighs, lapping at the rich outpourings of her well used cunt and tracing with her tongue the flares and welts the whips had left on her inner thighs.

There had been more but not that she could recall in any detail. And finally she had been hauled up and, squinting against the sun she had watched as a man had buckled her wrists into restraints nailed to the top of a whipping post. There was no set punishment tally by now. Any girl was fair game for as many as anyone cared to give her. Amelia knew that and even in her post-orgiastic state the knowledge gave her a further spurt of warmth in her groin. The wood of the post was warm on her cheek as she waited for anything further anyone wanted to do to her and thought she couldn't be happier. But then she realised that way down beneath all the pleasure of the uses to which she had been put, there was a part of her that was still wondering whether it might have been better to have made more use of Legs in the early events to extend the Girl Squad lead and trust in the girl's strength a bit more during later events. She groaned. Even here and even after all she had been through, she still wasn't the completely self-abandoned slave she had so wanted to be.

Up in the owners' box Angel sat up further in her seat as she felt Sadia's hand being withdrawn from her cunt, and she began to wriggle her short skirt back down her thighs. Beside her Tony finished coming in Eve's mouth and all three finally relaxed as the finale wound down. Craig Maddox and the Orange Team owner came across and formally congratulated them on a remarkable win. Angel grinned as Sadia proffered him her hand to kiss. It reeked of her vaginal secretions and he checked as he bowed over it but had no real choice other than to finish what he had started.

When they and their party had gone, they followed them down onto the arena floor. It was traditional that owners and trainers should take a bow at the end of an event and Angel in her leather skirt and leather waistcoat, straining across her breasts, got an extra big cheer.

She was feeling relaxed and happy. There would be money for more slaves now and their first home games could go ahead. And she had to admit that the aftermath of the finale was a fine sight. The ground seemed to be covered in panting and gasping female bodies, the full variety of female curves and valleys was on display and all of it bore the traces of every conceivable sort of pleasure having been taken from it. They might have been covered in dirt, smeared darker where the sweat ran, caked in sperm and cunt juice but they had a beauty all their own and she wished she could have had an easel and some paint to capture the debauched and depraved spectacle in all its glory. And for a fleeting moment she caught herself wondering how it would feel........Just then, Sadia gave a little cry and went across to a whipping post. Following her and stepping daintily over and around the bodies, Angel saw that she had found Ninety-seven, hanging by her wrists. Briskly Sadia ordered the girl to be released and to Angel's anger began to make a fuss of the creature, draping her limp form across her lap as she crouched at the foot of the post and wiping her face with her hankerchief.

"You see, Angel?" her mistress said, looking up happily. "I told you little Ninety-seven here would be our lucky talisman again!"

Angel could only grit her teeth and make no reply. She was still reeling from the fact that she had found herself wondering what it would be like to have been that carelessly used by so many and been beaten so joyfully by so many for their pleasure.

She had taken part in the finale to the first event the Girl Squad had fought, but by then there had been no points at stake so it had not been as hard fought as this. Now, something about the scale of the event and the harshness of the use was catching at her, making her breasts feel fuller and tighter against the leather of her waistcoat and beneath the short skirt, she was uncomfortably aware that she was wetter than Sadia's earlier attentions would account for.

And now this. A wretched cunt on legs was being credited with having won the event and Sadia was going all gooey over it, having it taken away and ordering the vet to look at it specially carefully. And even as Sadia returned to her and linked her arm in Angel's as they carefully trod their way towards the exit, she was looking towards where Nintey-seven was being carried away.

"That one is going to be very useful, Angel," she said.

"Yes, my lady," Angel managed, still grappling with the strange mixture of sensations she was feeling on the field of what should have been uncomplicated victory.

CHAPTER FOURTEEN

Carlo Suarez checked her girth and crupper, she was running with just a dildo today, but it was studded and he wanted to ensure she was getting good contact. It would be an insult to her greatness to get slack now, or to allow any slackness in her tack to creep in. He tugged at the strap where it split her labia, squeezing them out into plump cushions on either side of it, nestling the metal studs close against her inner flesh. She lifted one leg and pawed the ground with one of her decorative, hoof-like boots as he let the studs settle back. He checked the tit straps as well and then let her nuzzle his shoulder for a moment before he stepped over the shafts of the trap behind her, climbed aboard, unshipped his whip and just touched her up into 'Walk on.'

Her buttocks rolled as superbly as ever, he thought. They still bore their post-arena stripes, even though she had been at home for almost a week, but were none the worse for that. Her strong back flexed as she pulled him gently out from the CSL stableyard and onto the track that led through the woods, away from big house, past the assault course and the solitary confinement pit, then out onto the level tracks beyond the golf course, where the measured quarter mile lay for the racing ponies. He touched Blondie up again and she lifted smoothly into a trot as they entered the woods. The sun was slanting through the trees and her blonde hair and pale skin flickered through the bars of light.

"Whoa, girl," he called, easing back on the reins. They were coming to where the stream crossed the track and there was a shallow ford. She leaned back as the weight of the trap pushed her down the slope but then she leaned into her work again as the whip flicked her along, and she clattered through the water, gaining speed for the far bank. She dug in up the slope and crested the rise smoothly, hardly blowing at all and tossing her plumed bridle proudly. Then they were out of the woods and Carlo flicked her with the whip two, three times until she was fully into her graceful, high knee lift canter.

In only a few minutes' time he had a meeting with John Carpenter, Brian and Tony, Madame Stalevsky and Patti. They all knew what it was about. For the first time, the pillars that CSL's success had been built on had shown signs of cracking. Ayesha had not performed well and even Blondie had been bettered. He studied her back fondly and traced a pattern with the whip's tip on its satin skin. They were coming to the start of the measured quarter mile and Blondie knew it. She tossed her plumes and lifted her knees higher. Behind her Carlo smiled.

"Why not, girl, eh? Go!" He let fly with the whip and wrapped her ribs so the lash caught her across her strapped breasts. She reared up and arched her neck in delight. Her master was allowing her to gallop flat out on a fine morning. For a few minutes Carlo put his worries aside and just let Blondie do what she had done so well for so long.

In John's office they sat and waited in silence until Patti broke it.

"He'll be along, he just wanted to take Blondie for a drive…."

Everyone knew that Blondie was the most difficult problem facing them, but the other, only slightly lesser one was standing over by the windows. She was hooded and stood patiently, her weight on one leg, the other bent just slightly, her hands clipped together neatly behind her back and her long silken black hair in a pony tail coming from the back of the hood. Her tongue leash was hooked over an arm of a coat stand. From where Brian sat, her neat brand, the letters CSL set in a rectangle on her hip was caught by the sun. It didn't help matters to see it.

The door opened suddenly and Carlo entered, he took his seat right in front of John's desk, who called the meeting to order.

"We all know why we're here. At the Orange stable we got away with a victory through a combination of circumstances."

"And help from Amelia," Brian put in.

"Yes, it's odd how things turn out isn't it? But anyway, CSL still had a hand in a win, even if it wasn't how we planned it."

"I am not selling," Carlo growled.

"C'mon Carlo," Brian urged him. "Ayesha's never fully lived up to her billing since we got her. She's always been good, but never the superstar she was before – and we've never figured out why."

There was silence as everyone nodded. It was no more than the truth.

Carlo sighed. "I know," he said. "I didn't mean I wasn't going to sell, I meant I'm not putting any CSL stock on an auction block."

"Then how -?" Tony started.

"If you put CSL stock on an auction block, they look like any other livestock!" Carlo shouted suddenly. "And CSL stock is *not* like any other livestock!"

"I agree," Brian put in hastily. "We've built up an aura about our stock." They all glanced across at the graceful figure by the window, the long legs with the powerful forward curve of the thigh balancing the proud jut of the buttocks which curved into the sweep of the back. She was to die for.

"But she's not pulling her weight anymore," John Carpenter – owner of The Lodge and co-owner of CSL reminded them.

Carlo nodded glumly.

"So why don't we sell her by sealed tender," John suggested. "We circularise the whole arena market and the top end of the private market and ask for bids to be sent here. We'll open them with a solicitor present in.. let's say a month's time. Highest bid gets the prize!"

There were reluctant murmurs of assent. Everyone could see the sense of it, but it didn't address the main issue. If Ayesha could be sold – by whatever means – why couldn't Blondie? And if she wasn't going to be sold, then what was going to be done with her? Everyone knew Carlo was racking his brains and gave him space. Ayesha would realise enough to buy at least two new good prospects and probably pay for an extension to the stableblock. So there was that to look forward to in the short term. But everyone knew that it was only a matter of time before a decision had to be made.

Peter Lang opened the e mail and whistled in surprise. Then he sat back and looked around at the tropical splendour that lay just beneath the hotel terrace, it would be a wrench to cut short this well earned holiday but this was a prize well worth the winning. But it was a cunning way of selling and he would need to do some careful and tactful digging around. There was no guide price. So what sort of price might secure her? Who would be looking for a property like that? Who had a pocketful of money burning a hole in their pocket...... he whistled again and a wolfish grin spread across his features as he recalled the recent news from Indonesia.

Now there could be two prizes to be won if he pitched it right.......this would need careful handling indeed.

After all he had broken Ayesha to the bit straight off the streets as a bet with the prince, hadn't he? Why couldn't he consider another such challenge? And with two such specimens in his ownership, he could be at the start of something big. It was all in the preparation. He needed to know things and to talk to people who knew people who knew things. He had plenty of money, and even if money didn't actually talk, it encouraged speech in others and he was a good listener!

The one thing he needed above all was contact, face to face with her. If he could get that, he was confident he could break her in. And if she was interested in Ayesha, then that could be the way in he needed. He had to pull in every favour and make contact with every insider he could to find out if she was going to bid and, if so, how much.

He stood up abruptly and in half an hour was being driven to the only airport on the island.

On their return home, Angel had ordered the doors of the barracks to be left open all day for two days, and there was no training. The girls were given the use of their hands and were free to sleep with whoever they wanted, to shower, wash, groom – she had hairdressers bussed in – and to play, boxes of toys were left in each barrack block. By the third day, with marks fading, the dust of the Orange arena washed off and the glow of victory still strong, training resumed with gentle basic fitness regimes being re-established. From the Girl Squad's own arena, once more came the sound of hammering and welding as work began again to ready it for the upcoming home fixture.

With normality having been restored, Sadia attended Eric's club and was gone for two nights. She arrived back unannounced and as her car drove her across the training ground she saw a figure ankle suspended from a punishment frame in the centre of the ground. It was being subjected to a flogging from a long single tailed whip and was swaying back and forth under the lashes. It was a familiar figure and she ordered the driver to stop. As the car pulled over, the guard who had been delivering the beating with a stock whip came across.

"Who ordered this?" she demanded.

"Angel, my lady," the man replied.

"What offence?"

The man shrugged.

"Where's Angel now?"

"Out with half the squad on a run."

"Take her down and bring her to me!"

The man looked uncomfortable to be caught in the middle of a disagreement between the owner and trainer but nodded.

Seated in her chair by the balcony of her office, Sadia sipped her drink and tried to calm down. What on earth was Angel doing disciplining the best slave they had so severely?

She rang her mobile.

"Ever since we got back the little bitch's been giving me the eye!" Angel said when Sadia protested about Ninety-seven's treatment. "Dumb insolence! Nothing else! She thinks she's god's gift to this stable and I'm going to break her in properly, she'll bloody well learn her place if it's the last thing I do!"

Quite suddenly it occurred to Sadia that Angel had not been the lover she had been before the games, and added to that, Eric said there had been informal approaches from several other trainers following the

Girl Squad's successful entry into the arena world. She resisted the urge to say that it could well be the last thing she did. This needed calm thought and not rash action.

"Angel you know as well as I do that an over-beaten slut goes sullen and resentful! That's not what we need. We'll talk more when you get back."

She broke the connection as there was a knock on the door and the guard entered, half carrying a dizzy and well-whipped Ninety-seven. She waved him away, back over to the door and the slave dropped onto all fours, leaving dust and dirt marks on the immaculate dark wood floor.

"Come!" Sadia ordered and extended an elegantly shod foot. The slave crawled forwards, kissed it and knelt back, thighs apart, hands on knees, eyes cast down.

"Angel tells me you've been making eye contact with her. Have you?"

The slave shook her head and Sadia reached out and took the girl's chin, tilting it up, making her look at her.

"It's alright, I won't punish you," she said, looking into Ninety-seven's dark eyes and seeing nothing but puzzlement there

Sadia took a close look at the girl. She had been soundly flogged – and not in one session by the look of it. The skin was close to breaking in places and lines of welts crossed others at flanks, buttocks, ribs and breasts.

"How many times has this one been punished?" she demanded angrily.

"Yesterday. Day before, and the day before that, after you left," the guard said.

Sadia sat back and looked at the mutely kneeling slave.

"Take her to the vet. Have her kept in the sick bay until further orders!"

"Yes, my lady." The man came forward and helped Ninety-seven to her feet with a little more care than Sadia felt he would have shown a few minutes previously.

An hour later Angel strode into the office with a print-off in her hand.

"Where've you been?" Sadia demanded. "I saw the squad come back half an hour ago!"

Angel waved her hand impatiently. "Never mind that! Look at this! I want her!" and she plonked the paper down on Sadia's desk. Sadia was too surprised at how completely her complaint at Ninety-seven's treatment had been brushed aside to protest and glanced down to see the mail advertising that CSL were inviting sealed bids for Ayesha.

"She really didn't do very well in Indonesia," Sadia observed.

"She's not being handled right!" Angel strode up and down past the desk. "Give her to me for two months and I'll have the bitch motivated alright. You can see it in her eyes. She doesn't care anymore! Carlo's gone soft!"

"Well…." Sadia said playing for time. "I'll talk to Eric about it."

"And that's another thing! Why do we need him now? We can run our own show, we've proved that and you can get rid of those bloody tags he put on you!"

Angel paced over to the window and glanced down at the training ground.

"Oh for God's sake, you had the little cow taken down?! Well it's *my* job to decide who gets flogged how much and when! Discipline is the trainer's job, you just make sure I've got the money to do it properly!" She marched out and slammed the door behind her.

"Well, well," Sadia said softly, staring at the door. "I think our Angel's got just a bit of a high opinion of herself all of a sudden. I think I might need to talk to nice Uncle Eric about her....."

"Now isn't that interesting!" It was two days later and Eric's voice came out of the speaker on Sadia's desk. There had simply been shouting matches between owner and trainer in the intervening days and Sadia had had to content herself with having slaves sent to her bed. She had forbidden Ninety-seven to be released back into Angel's jurisdiction and Angel was still seething. The squad was being punished rather than trained and Sadia was becoming increasingly alarmed.

"I've had someone on the phone only this morning asking if you might be interested in bidding," Eric went on. "And you say Angel wants her?"

"Angel is being quite impossible!" Sadia replied. "She's insisting our little Ninety-seven - Amelia, remember I told you about her, she more or less won that last event for us – is being insolent and she had her hung up and whipped day in and day out while I was away, it's as if she's jealous!"

"Hmm. It sounds like the Girl Squad might need a new trainer. You can't get personal when you've got a stable to run."

"Well I'm going right off her! And if I'm not careful she'll ruin the whole squad. So if you can find someone else and get rid of her, that's fine by me!"

"I think I might be able to – let's say – make life a little difficult for Angel at the least, and then we'll see what we'll see. I'll need to know what she wants to bid."

Sadia told him and he whistled. "She needs to go now, Sadia, she'll bankrupt you at that rate. But if she's going that far over the top, it plays into our hands. I'll make a few calls."

"Thank you dahling," Sadia purred. "I'll see you at the club next week. Can we put that blonde piece through a real session this time. I'm sure she can take a lot more than she's been getting."

"For you Sadia, we'll make a pin cushion of her!"

Eric put the phone down and punched the air. That Angel bitch had just signed her freedom away, if he was any judge of things, and that meant that Sadia would be free to concentrate on him. He picked up the phone once more and dialled.

"Peter, I've got good news for you. I can give you the figure you need. Match it and I don't think anyone else will be in the running. Added to that her mistress wants to dump her, so she's up for grabs alright – just doesn't know it. Yet."

John Carpenter looked at the two pieces of paper incredulously.

"We've had over two hundred bids! What are the odds on two coming in exactly the same to the last penny?"

Carlo shrugged. All he was concerned about was the size of the two bids. Whichever was settled on, he could build a new, bigger stable block and add three new slaves. And probably have some small change! For the first time in weeks he was feeling happy.

"So how do we decide on whether to take Peter Lang's bid or Angel Smythe's?"

"Well," Carlo said slowly as an idea occurred to him. "They both want her, let them compete against each other to get her."

He explained his idea to John.

CHAPTER FIFTEEN

Angel slung her case out of the car and stared around. She had never been to Scotland before. Gillhoolie House, surrounded by thickly wooded hills, rivers and lakes, was set almost ten miles from the nearest town and stood in the middle of its own huge estate. It was also owned by one of the members of The Lodge – as Carlo had told her when he had phoned her to explain how they were going to work a tie break.

She picked up her case and walked into the huge, granite porch and from there into the main hall, whose walls were haunted by the heads of dead stags, boar and otter.

A polite enough maid, a young woman dressed demurely in knee length black skirt and crisp white shirt, showed her to her room and when she had freshened up she went down for dinner.

As she showered she reflected that Sadia was behaving very oddly. Firstly she had flagrantly interfered with her running of the stable over that little bitch, then she had suddenly caved in regarding the bid for Ayesha and released the Ninety-seven creature back into her hands, where her punishment had been able to continue properly while she got on with running the rest of the bitches.

For all she knew, Sadia would have the insolent little cow in her bed by now. Well, let her! If she could get her hands on Ayesha – and get what she was really capable of out of her – Sadia could keep her little harem. She would be the trainer they would all want! Maybe the Prince of Bakhtar himself would want her. Now there was a man who understood discipline!

By the time she was finished and had gone downstairs she was feeling much happier.

Apart from the serving staff, she was the only female present but that was something she was well used to. She recognised Carlo of course but the tall, spare, suntanned man who was talking to him over a drink as she entered the library was not so familiar. Then with a shock she realised it was Peter Lang who had been the trainer of the Prince of Bakhtar's stable until recently. She wondered how much he resented her part in what she supposed was his downfall. The men stood beside the fireplace, which was unlit on this late spring evening, beneath an impressive painting of moors and grouse being put up.

Carlo smiled at her as she approached. She had been expecting a male domain and had dressed accordingly, she was wearing a long, clinging dress that was cut quite high at the neck but which was dramatically split up to her left hip, leaving the leg to flash its nudity tantalisingly as she walked. She wore no bra and without looking, knew that her breasts shook and swung in a man-bewitching way as well. Carlo knew the trick though and kept eye contact with her until he was able to introduce Peter, who made no attempt to disguise his admiration of her body.

They shook hands and Carlo summoned a different maid to fetch her a glass of wine.

"When Ralph joins us," Carlo said, "we'll explain exactly how this hunt will work."

"I'd like to see the quarry," she said.

"Do you think I might've nobbled her?" Lang asked with laconic amusement.

"I have my reasons!" she snapped.

Carlo made a conciliatory gesture and summoned the maid.

"Show Angel to the stables, let her examine the goods in any way she wants," he said.

She was guided outside and had to hold her dress up off the cobbles as they crossed a stableyard and entered the stables. She was impressed. Whoever this Ralph was he knew his girlflesh.

No fewer than six ponies were stabled and were being attended to by a brunette with thick hair held back off her face by an Alice band. She had a shirt and jeans on and filled both very well, Angel noticed as they smiled and nodded at each other.

"She's been here since Tuesday, the maid told her," leading her to the far end of the stalls. "They've not had her out at all and she's getting pretty restive."

Ayesha was prowling up and down her stall, the chain that locked her right ankle to the wall at the back, clinking and slithering. Angel let herself in and immediately went to the slave's right leg; it was the one she had damaged in the chariot smash.

A smack on the flank made the slave lift her foot obediently as Angel bent and examined the leg, bending and flexing it, twisting it and listening for any gasps of pain. She seemed sound enough. Had there been any weakness, Angel wanted to know about it. If they were to hunt her, then it might make all the difference. – especially if she knew something that Peter Lang didn't.

Satisfied, but disappointed that there didn't seem to be damage only she knew about, she let herself out and the maid led her back. The groom stopped what she was doing and gave Angel a blatantly lascivious stare as they approached. Angel stopped and went close to the girl, who stood her ground.

"Where've they put you?" she asked Angel.

Angel was intrigued and taken aback by the girl's lack of any compunction about making such an obvious move.

"Oh, don't worry," she said, seeing Angel's surprise. "Daddy knows I do pretty much what I like when I'm home."

"First floor, third door along on the left of the landing."

The girl nodded. "Go and do what you've got to with the men. I'll drop by later." She tossed her thick hair and smiled brightly, winked and went back to work.

Angel felt the evening suddenly held a lot more promise than it had a few minutes earlier. But she wanted to get things just a little clearer and she caught the arm of the maid walking ahead of her in her demure uniform as they crossed the yard.

"She's the daughter of the owner, right?" she asked.

"Miss Sara is the laird's oldest daughter, yes," the woman told her calmly.

"And he doesn't mind who she shags?"

The woman flinched from the crudity. "Miss Sara follows in the family tradition of doing pretty much what she wants," she said, and for the first time a slight smile crossed her face. Suddenly Angel realised that the woman was not unattractive, despite her rather conservative dress. And of course this laird was a member of The Lodge.

"And he does pretty much what he wants with you?"

The woman inclined her head. "Pretty much," she agreed and went inside the main house. Angel followed, intrigued but determined not to be distracted. There was work to do after all.

Ralph Lockhart was a powerfully built man with a florid complexion and a full head of brown hair – like father like daughter, Angel thought. And over an excellent dinner of langoustine and a cold collation of locally reared beef and venison, he explained the rules of the hunt.

A board was brought in with an Ordnance Survey map pinned to it.

"As you'll see, the estate is bordered to the north by this lake here…..and by this river to the West. The rest of the perimeter is bounded by eight foot high fences with razor wire for the top two feet and CCTV is in operation. I have no desire to allow anyone to see what goes on in here!" He paused and grinned at the maid who was topping up the wine glasses.

She blushed and curtsied.

"I believe Angel has seen my stable," he went on. "Some of the finest stock north of the border. So back to business, there is no chance the quarry can escape. She will have exactly what you will have except for the binoculars we've provided for you. Water, sleeping bag, simple rations. She's been told she has to stay free of both of you for two days, if she can, she's been promised she'll have Purdy in her stall for a week. After that, if that happens, she'll be put out to tender again. All you have to do is subdue her and lead her in. It's up to you to decide for yourselves whether you attempt to wrest her from the other on the way back. All Carlo is concerned about is that she is captured and paid for. Whatever happens out there is up to you. She goes to whoever leads her back to this house. We will make one concession however. If we haven't seen either of you making any progress by the day after tomorrow, we might have a drive and put her up. Then leave it you to bring her down."

Angel looked across at Peter Lang who seemed almost insultingly relaxed.

"Do we start off from the same place?" she asked.

"No. The quarry will be released at a secret location an hour before you start. And you'll start from completely different locations."

It seemed quite straightforward. Angel had always made her way in a man's world and knew she was as fast and as tough as some men. Was more cunning than most and was utterly determined that Ayesha would be hers. Already she could envisage her 'inbox' filling up with enquiries about her services when, with Ayesha properly restored to her brilliant best, her Girl Squad had carried all before it at the first home fixture.

The rest of the meal passed with normal male conversation and Angel joined in occasionally but her heart wasn't in it. It rarely was, she was thinking more of the full lips and succulent figure of the laird's daughter. She stayed for one glass of brandy and noted that the tray it was delivered on to Ralph, apart from bottle and glasses had that most Scottish of implements on it; a tawse.

She was happy to leave the men to their amusements with the domestic staff, in fact she hoped that Lang would make a real night of it!

In her room she slipped out of her dress and knickers, slipped under the duvet and turned the light off. She was tired in any case, so even if the girl didn't show up, she would get her sleep.

In fact she was woken in the dark by the feel of soft hair tickling her back and she felt the mattress sink slightly. There was a waft of expensive perfume and then the feel of breasts against her back and of a belly against her buttocks. Then the girl was curled up, spoon-like against her back and her hands were roving gently across Angel's stomach and chest, feeling for the weight and curve of her own breasts, seeking the nipples.

Soft lips kissed her shoulder.

"So tell me, Angel, what's it like to have sooo many bitches to whip and fuck and do whatever you want to?"

Angel reached behind her and felt the warm, graceful curve of a female waist and hip and she smiled in the dark. Well she would sleep all the more soundly for a little pleasure.....

She twisted onto her back and spread her legs.

"Lick me out and I'll tell you all about it," she whispered back.

"Oh, we can do better than that!" the girl returned, giggling. There was rustling and movement beside her and Angel felt the girl's breath caress her thighs, while her own thighs settled on the pillow beside Angel's face, the pungent fragrance of her cunt filling Angel's nostrils.

"I'll tell you later!" she said and buried her face between her invisible lover's legs.

It was much later when she did, but she slept well and was fresh for the hunt the next morning.

CHAPTER SIXTEEN

Angel hefted her pack onto her back and looked around as the Jeep lurched off back down the track. All round her was a fir plantation. She thought for a moment and then headed uphill. She reckoned she needed to see how the land lay. It had looked a pretty big piece of land on the map and Ayesha could be anywhere. The sun was warm so her nakedness wouldn't be a factor yet, but she would probably go for cover somewhere where she could hear or see pursuit coming.

A fir plantation could be perfect, but they wouldn't have dropped her right on top of the quarry would they? But how would they know? Thoughts whirled through Angel's mind as she started off uphill anyway.

Her feet slipped sometimes on the mat of pine needles that covered the ground, the air was hot and still and she was soon sweating. But after only half an hour or so, she broke out and found herself at the top of the hill overlooking the lake and open country beyond. She sat down and took the binoculars out then surveyed everything before her. Apart from some cattle she could see nothing moving. The far perimeter was just in sight, so the task of finding Ayesha was not impossible and perhaps it was best to keep to the high ground and keep watchful. She kept her eyes glued to the binoculars and swept across a promisingly open piece of parkland just South of the house.

And there, just at the edge of a small copse she caught a glimpse of something – of course! The bitch was naked, she wouldn't want to go into heavy cover where there could be briars and nettles. She was sure she had seen a flash of olive skin. She was so intent that she never heard a thing and by the time her head cleared it was far too late.

Lang poured some cold water over her face and squatted down so she could see him clearly as she blinked her head clear. He let her examine how she was tied. She was lying on her face with her legs parted and her ankles bound behind a tree trunk. Her arms were likewise pulled behind her and bound to the same tree. She was also naked.

He watched as all these realisations were borne in on her.

Then he went to a bag and took from it a heavy and bitterly sharp hunting knife, she assumed it was the one he had used to slice her clothing away, then he took out a hood, a collar and a lead.

"Just so there is no misunderstanding. Any duplicity is entirely mine Angel. I was trained in a part of the army that places heavy emphasis on self-reliance so I made sure I knew where, when and how this was being arranged. Then I also made sure I had all the winning cards. I came here a couple of nights ago and left this little bag of goodies ready to be dug up."

He sat down in front of her. "Ask me any questions you want to. In a moment I shall deprive you of speech – amongst other things – and I would like you to know what is being done to you."

Angel struggled against her bonds in involuntary panic but there was no give anywhere.

"W...why?" she whimpered. She was alone in an isolated place with a man who had very little reason to like her. And he was a man who had jumped her, tied her and now had a very large knife in his hand.

"Angel, I shall walk back to the house with both you and Ayesha on leashes. Ayesha I can have eating out of my hand at any time; believe me. That means I am free to concentrate on you."

"You can't! I won't!" Despair made her voice stronger and with a sudden inspiration, she screamed as loudly as she could, and went on screaming until she was hoarse. Lang didn't move.

He waited till she had choked to a stop. "No one on this estate bats an eyelid when a girl screams," he chortled. "The laird is partial to outdoor pursuits I believe. And now if there are no further questions, we'll begin. I haven't got as much time as I'd like but I think it will suffice."

He picked up the hood and moved towards Angel who tried ineffectually to jerk her head away. It was a thick and stern affair with heavy pads over eyes and ears and a mouth piece that could be zipped completely shut, but there were also press studs that could be undone to allow some breathing. Only at the nostrils were there any holes that couldn't be closed off. He lowered it gently over her head as she whimpered and pleaded and then buckled it firmly about her neck, not too tightly of course. Just firmly enough so that her darkness was complete.

He had had to adapt his technique to suit the circumstances once he had learned how the hunt was to be conducted, but he didn't think that Angel would present too many problems. He had a hunch that she was farther along the road he wanted to take her down that anyone, including herself, knew. He stood back and let her breathing calm down as she accepted the inevitability of the hood and then he carefully untied her and helped her to her feet. Even cowed and huddled, she was a splendid looking woman. A real adornment to a man – and she was going to be. There was no doubt about that. Back in Bakhtar he had used the dark of the passages behind the old fort to lead Ayesha through until she was broken in. But as he had stalked Angel up here, and on his reconnaissance visit, he had seen enough of the country to believe that he could take her on a wild enough ride.

He came close to her and touched her upper arm. She jumped, the hood was doing its job perfectly. He fed the collar round her neck and buckled it as well. It wasn't so important to his immediate plans but he knew it would disturb her, and he wanted her disturbed. He had left her hands tied behind her and now took the leash, clipped the karabiner over the rope that bound her wrists and passed it between her legs. She shied and shivered, tried to jerk away and succeeded, only to trip backwards and sprawl on the grass – her head inches away from a fallen log. Angrily he hauled her up and unzipped part of one ear pad.

"Don't be so bloody stupid! If you do as I say, no harm will come to you. Fight me and I may not be able to help you. There are steep paths and sheer drops on this estate and I will tell you when you are balanced on the edge of one! Trust me and I will bring you safely home. Panic and you might fall!"

Angel stood stock still as the import of his words sank in. She had seen crags and streams away to her right when she had sat with the binoculars. The extent of her peril was becoming ever more real to her and Peter Lang smiled as he took up her lead, gathered his pack and his bag, stuck his knife in his belt, selected a sharp stick that would seem to her, when she felt it on her skin, to be a large, heavy, steel hunting knife – she had seen it hadn't she? – and whistling quietly through his teeth he led her slowly on what was going to be the longest journey of her life.

Utterly lost and sobbing in terror, Angel gingerly shuffled one foot in front of the other, feeling nothing worse than grass and twigs under her feet. The lead rubbed against her inner thighs. The air was cool on her goose bumped skin and she tried desperately to recall where she was, had there been any sheer drops? Any dangers that he could be leading her into. And why was he doing this anyway? To break her into being a slave like Ayesha, he had said. That was ridiculous, she was dominant – always had been! – but just at the moment she did have to admit that the bastard was holding all the aces. Perhaps she had better go along with whatever he wanted, until the lunatic returned her to the house. Then she could get help! Carlo wouldn't let this happen! Ralph Lockhart wouldn't let this happen either. Her thoughts shuddered to a halt. As long as money changed hands, who cared about the slaves? As long as they were kept healthy of course! But that was what her world was founded on and now she was at the bottom of the heap. A prisoner, held naked and vulnerable at the mercy of a man who seemed terrifyingly confident in his ability to do whatever he wanted with her. But somewhere there must be someone who would help her. She just had to endure until they turned up.

Angel felt the ground slope down more steeply and tried to mumble through the mouthpiece, to whimper and beg. Where was she being taken?

At last she felt his hand on her arm and for a fleeting second was grateful for the contact. One ear pad was unzipped slightly and the press studs across her mouth.

"Do you trust me?" Lang's voice whispered close beside her.

For a moment she almost burst into hysterical laughter. Was he mad? But common sense kicked in just in time.

"Oh yes!" she gushed. "Yes, and you can trust me too. Just let me see and I won't make a sound I promise!" Never had sight seemed so important as it did now in the Stygian black, leather smelling claustrophobic darkness.

He laughed and his touch was gone and the pads were refastened.

She felt a tug on her leash and a sharp point touched her ribs. Her mind filled with images of the huge knife she had seen him heft. Sobbing she felt ahead of her with one foot. The ground seemed alright. She slid her other foot up to it and felt ahead again. It felt like wood now. Narrow, just about as wide as her foot. She felt wind against her skin and the ear pad was undone a little. She heard water. How far beneath her was it?

"Don't worry," he whispered. "I won't let you fall if you follow me." Again the leash was tugged and she shuffled on. The wood trembled and she screamed. His hand was on her arm again.

"Two more paces, Angel. I won't allow you to fall."

She sobbed again, seeing in her mind's eye the tumbling waters of a mountain stream rushing below her, she had seen them on the way up here. This must be some kind of fragile plank he had rigged up to terrify her. Well it was working, she felt as if she would wet herself as she slid her foot forward again and then again and then there was grass under her feet. Her sobs turned to laughter and she would have collapsed to her knees if she had dared.

So far so good, Peter thought as he watched her. He kept hold of the leash and went forward to stroke her for a bit. The plank she had crossed was two feet long and three feet above the water, her own mind had done the rest. But working to her logic he needed to congratulate her and reinforce the fact that no matter what danger she was in; he wouldn't let her fall.

For Angel the torment was an eternity. The noise of her blood and her breathing filled her ears. Timidly she followed the insistent pull between her legs. When the urge to pee got too bad she stopped and refused to move. He took the leash from between her legs and with his hand led her to somewhere where she was made to squat. For all she knew there could have been thousands of grinning spectators and for a long time her bladder refused to work. But once it had, to add to her complete humiliation, she felt him dry her with some leaves, before he stood her up, passed the lead between her legs and led her on. They went uphill at times and at others they seemed to be on the level but always she proceeded at a terrified shuffle.

Then at last she was allowed to kneel. Her leash was dropped and she was able to relish the relative security of not having to move forwards into darkness. She gathered that he was moving about, from time to time she would feel faint vibrations in the ground beside her, sometimes there would be a brush of cloth against her.

Then finally, just as she was about to shiver, she felt warmth. He had lit a fire. Soon he came to sit beside her and unzipped her mouth covering and one ear pad. Then he fed her from his hand. She was too exhausted from fear to complain and at least if he was feeding her it meant he wasn't about to do anything terrible to her. Didn't it?

When she was feeling a little better, he helped her to come a little closer to the fire. She heard it crackling, quite close. She tried to hang back.

"Trust me, Angel!" he urged her. "If not I'll have to punish you!"

A storm of revolt flared up in her. He was not going to punish her! How dare he! She wasn't some subby bitch cowering before her master, she shook free of his grip for a second and threw herself back onto the cool grass. His hand was around her ankle instantly.

"Now I will have to!" he said quietly.

Wriggling and writhing as best she could, she fought him until she was bound to a tree with her ankles secured to the trunk and her hands wrenched up behind her, making her bend forwards. Her breasts hung full and vulnerable beneath her. He stroked and caressed them to underline that point. Suddenly it seemed to Angel as if there were no more fear she could feel. She crumbled into abject crying as she knew that whatever he was going to do to her poor breasts, there was nothing she could do about it.

She felt a growing warmth come towards her chest. She screamed as a source of heat came closer and closer. She tugged at her bonds and begged for mercy. Then there was an appalling, blinding pain at her left nipple and she reared in despair and panic. But it came again at her right nipple. Horror after horror fled through her shattered mind. What had he done to her?

There was absolute stillness and as she calmed, a new sensation filtered through into her brain. Her nipples were dripping something cold. She sagged in her bonds and shamelessly let her bladder go. She had done similar things in dungeons before. Mindfucking helpless subs into believing that what they were feeling was intense heat when in fact it was just an ice cube. Lang must have soaked something in a stream to chill it, then with one hand held a taper and with the other touched her with something cold.

"Why!?" she groaned as she felt him clean her up again and then release her and bring her back to kneel by the fire.

He unzipped her ear pad more fully.

"Because you must trust me. Every slave must trust her master absolutely."

"I'm not your bloody slave! I'm nobody's slave!"

"Not yet," he agreed calmly. "But you're not really a dominant are you?"

"What do you mean?" It came out more petulantly and more sharply then she had meant and for a second she cringed in case he punished her again.

He laughed softly. "No, I'm not going to punish you. But you haven't been honest have you? I've always seen it in you. Tell me about subs and slaves. You like them don't you?"

The direction of the conversation was so unexpected it was a blessed relief.

"Yes," she conceded. "I like the way their bodies move when I play with them. I like to watch them come when I beat them or use needles."

"You like their pain?"

"I like the way they enjoy the pain and the way some can't get enough of being humiliated."

"You've been humiliated today. Did you like it?"

Angel was stopped in her tracks. She had been reduced to a stumbling wreck behind this man, she had pissed in front of him, he had cleaned her up. And every touch of his hand had been heavenly relief from the isolation of the hood.

"No!" she shook her head furiously.

He laughed in that irritating, quiet way of his and she realised she was listening to him more closely than she had ever listened to anyone before. She was hearing his breathing, she had noticed the way his breath caught just a little before he spoke. The timbre of his voice was deeper and more relaxed than it had been.

"How do you know you're a domme, Angel?"

That at least was easy.

It had been at school. Her parents were abroad – as always – and hadn't been able to get back to pick her up form boarding school at the end of the summer term in her final year before university.

The school hadn't minded her staying on for a few days and she had enjoyed herself, swimming, running, working out in the gym and having the television all to herself in the evenings.

One day she had been showering off after coming back from a run when Miss Lukins had walked in, quite naked and taken the shower opposite her.

"You don't mind do you Angela?" she had asked. "Only they've turned our showers off for the holidays and I've just had a run too."

Miss Lukins was one of the more popular teachers, a fresh-faced graduate in political history whose enthusiasm for her subject would turn out to have helped Angel to an A grade.

They had dressed and chatted and gradually Angel's shyness had evaporated. Of course she was perfectly used to being naked with her fellow students, although she had never indulged in some of the after-lights-out under the blankets explorations that she knew did go on from time to time. Miss Lukins was that bit fuller figured, her hips were broader than most of the girls, certainly broader than Angel's at that time and Angel was fascinated by her breasts. They were not the flabby, doughy things that some of the fat girls had, nor were they the oversized melons that some girls sported for a brief few years in adolescence. They were enticingly large with dark red areola but stood proud and firm on her chest. Angel's were still developing and she was frankly envious. With all the rampant hormonal drives of her age, she made no attempt to resist Miss Lukins' line in chat up, which ended with a dinner invitation at her rooms that night.

"But I've not got much to wear apart from school uniform," she had protested naively.

Miss Lukins had smiled and told her to just come as she pleased.

The rest of the afternoon had passed in a frenzy of trying on and throwing off until finally she had settled on a pink T shirt that was just a little small but which therefore made her breasts look a bit more grown up, worn over a short, dark skirt. She went bare legged as it had been a reasonable summer and she was quite tanned. The best she could do in shoes was a pair of heeled sandals that another of the prefects had left behind.

Miss Lukins answered the door dressed in a yellow shirt and a pale green skirt that was tailored and stopped a good four inches above the knee. The afternoon in the changing room hadn't prepared her for how shapely and smooth Miss Lukins legs were. With her heart thundering she allowed herself to be led in, her only thought was one of relief that Miss Lukins had never shown herself off like this in class; there wouldn't have been a dry seat in the room.

Even looking back on it, Angel could never really say if she expected to go to bed with Miss Lukins or not. Or whether she had expected to be seduced or whether she wanted to lose her virginity to another woman. She only knew that Miss Lukins was smart and sexy and talked to her like an adult and she wanted to find out more about…..about everything. Men and women. Why all the local boys just wanted to get their hands up her skirt? When if they behaved more like men, she would have begged them to put their hands up there and feel her. And now here she was with an adult who seemed to like her and who seemed so relaxed about everything.

They ate they talked and they drank. Miss Lukins kept making arch comments about not wanting to get her drunk. And Angel didn't have that much, but it was enough.

At last, Miss Lukins had got up from the table. Put some music on low and beckoned Angel to come and join her on the sofa. By this time there was no pretence. Angel was eighteen after all and somehow two of Miss Lukins buttons had come undone and the valley of her cleavage was showing.

She sat back as Angel – even though she was desperately looking forward to whatever was going to happen – sat awkwardly beside her, balancing on the front of the sofa, not quite able to relax back.

Miss Lukins laughed. "Come here, Angela," she said and held out an arm. Hesitantly, knowing this was supposed to be happening with a man but absolutely dying to know what it would be like with a woman, Angel let herself be cradled by the arm as she sat back, half turned towards her teacher.

"You couldn't keep your eyes off them this afternoon," Miss Lukins said, squinting down at her chest. "Want another look?"

"Oh yes, please Miss – I mean Anne."

With trembling fingers, Angel had undone her shirt and helped her shrug it back off her shoulders and with some more giggling struggles get rid of it entirely. Then there had been a time of slow, wondering stroking, Angel loving the pleasure she was giving and savouring the size and firmness of mature breasts.

There was no hurry now. The spell was cast. They would go the whole way.....when it pleased them. Anne's bra was taken off and Angel kissed her nipples, laughing as they hardened to a size far in excess of her little nubs. Anne got up to put another CD on, letting her breasts sway freely. Angel stood up and took off her T shirt and bra so that when Anne came back they could rub their breasts together and she so wanted Anne's hands on them.

When Anne's hand began to slide up her thigh and under her skirt, it was so assured and so unlike the frantic explorations of the local boys that Angel had simply parted her legs and lain back while her lover had expertly aroused her without even taking her knickers off. Then she had leaned forwards and kissed her so deeply that Angel thought the top of her head would come off.

"Let's go to bed and get those off there," she had said at last.

Angel had never been able to forget the thrill of putting her fingers into Anne. But then she had never forgotten the thrill of feeling Anne probing inside her, finding her hymen and then producing a sizable vibrator from the bedside table.

"Want to get rid of it?"

At that moment, Angel would have sold her soul if Anne had asked her to. The loss of her virginity, if it meant that Anne was free to penetrate her as deeply as she wanted to, was a paltry thing.

Angel stuttered, gasped, trembled and twitched her way to the stars so many times that night it was getting light before sleep overtook them. She even fell asleep with her face between Anne's legs.

In the morning they shared a bath and compared how much each of them stung in the aftermath and soaped every nook and cranny of each other's body. They ate breakfast naked and licked yoghurt off each other's nipples. Then they sucked it out of each other's cunt. After that they had another bath.

In the days that followed Anne drove them away from town in the evenings so they could go to dinner without being spotted. They stopped the car on the way home and played at boy friends trying to get off with them in the back seat. Angel would try and get her hand up Anne's skirt by distracting her with outrageous claims to have seen UFOs and little green men. Furious wrestling matches ensued that rocked the car in the lay by. Then Angel would pretend to sulk and Anne would placate her by putting Angel's hand inside her blouse or spreading her legs and letting her feel about until they needed to get home and get the toys out.

It was still a time that Angel looked back on as being the happiest of her life. But then came the morning that changed everything.

Anne was quiet. Angel's parents were coming to collect her in two days' time. Angel was determined to cram every second full of experimentation and excitement but Anne sat her down in the small kitchen of her flat and told her that a lot of people would think she had behaved terribly badly.

Angel had protested. But Anne had been insistent, Angel was young, she shouldn't have been pushed into it so quickly. She, Anne, was to blame.

Angel had gone on protesting until Anne had taken her face in her hands and kissed her until she melted.

"Will you help me feel better?" she asked. Angel nodded.

"Then punish me and I'll feel I've paid for my bad behaviour."

Angel had no idea what she meant but was willing to do anything to bring back the happy, lovestruck Anne.

Taking her hand, Anne led her into the bedroom and knelt down, feeling about under the bed.

"Teachers always used to have these you know! But they used to use them on naughty girls.......so you'll have to use it on this naughty girl."

She stood up brandishing a cane and handed it to an astonished Angel.

Anne went to the chair that stood in front of her dressing table and turned it so the back was facing her, then she hitched up her skirt and wrenched down her knickers before bending over the back and holding onto the sides of the seat.

"I think six for a first offence, Angel. But I daresay I'll need more tomorrow, I think I'm going to be very naughty tonight." She gave Angel a look of lascivious invitation. "I think I might be tempted to rim you tonight and that would be very naughty indeed!"

Angel was staring at her lover's bottom. She adored the smooth curves and the silky skin but having it offered to her to hit seemed terrible and wonderful all at the same time. They had scratched at each other as they had rolled in their passion and the pain had heightened the passion. This must be an extension of the same thing.

"Don't be afraid, Angel. It makes a loud noise and hurts terribly. But I want it to. I like the hurt, Angel. Do it for me!"

And Angel had beaten her lover. Hard. It had come naturally.

When the swishing and smacking, the most exciting things Angel had ever heard had fallen silent and a sniffling Anne had slowly stood up, her mentor had fallen to her knees in front of her and kissed her hands again and again in gratitude.

Angel had loved the way the shockwaves had run through the soft flesh of the buttocks each time they were struck, she had loved how Anne had wriggled and cried but had not attempted to rise. It was the sexiest thing she had ever seen.

And in bed that night, after an exquisite meal out, for which Anne had refused to wear knickers; 'I want to go on feeling everything my darling gave me!" she had been a demon in bed. Before that night she had been a gentle, if raunchy angel. That night and for the few left to them, she had been a down and dirty whore who had introduced Angel to the delights of anal sex. She had displayed a streak of exhibitionism that left Angel breathless. Driving the car home naked one night, she had got out at an all night station and gone to the toilet, then walked calmly back across the forecourt under full floodlights. Her bottom was constantly marked. The canings increased until on their final night together a climactic total of twenty strokes was dished out over the evening.

CHAPTER SEVENTEEN

"And you never saw her again?" Lang asked her when she finished.

"A couple of times we met while I was at uni and we had good times in some hotels. But then she moved to Manchester and got involved in the scene there. I lost touch."

"So you immediately understood the connection between pleasure and pain?"

"Yes."

"I wonder. Goodnight."

Abruptly the ear pad was closed and her mouth was zipped up. She felt him walk away and then he returned with a sleeping bag that he spread out on the ground, he helped her into it and zipped her into that as well, effectively imprisoning her as her hands were still bound.

Angel had no way of knowing whether he was standing over her in the firelight, looking down at her, contemplating whatever it was he going to do with her, or whether he was asleep on the other side of the fire. Her thoughts ran on and on. What had he meant about 'I wonder' when she had said she had instantly understood and responded to the relationship between pain and pleasure.

The sight of Anne's bottom so eagerly presented for the cane played itself again and again in the darkness of the hood. She began to drift into a troubled doze. In her dreams Lang was standing above her, she could see him and he was a giant figure towering over her. But she wanted him there, she didn't want to be alone. Then it wasn't Lang, it was Anne who shook a cane at her and told her she had been a bad girl and she had to bend over. And with the thought of bending over and being caned by Anne came peace and she slept.

Peter Lang had waited until she was quite still before walking softly over and standing over her. She had come along beautifully. Better than he had expected. In a day's time he would lead her on a leash back to the house with Ayesha.

He hand fed her breakfast and she made no protest. He led her to the bushes to perform her functions and she stayed patiently still while he cleaned her up.

Then he led her off. He made her wade through ice cold water, never knowing if the next step would plunge her into a hole up to her neck, or worse, would result in her being swept away. And always when she broke and couldn't make another move into the dark; he was there. Insisting, leading, touching, goading just a little. By early afternoon he had the lead passed over one shoulder and was whistling happily as he strolled along. Behind him came the naked Angel, now walking almost unafraid. He led her over more planks and across streams that sounded like gorges to her. He led her to outcrops of rock and had her stand at their brinks, while he stood in front of her, just below her and when he was ready picked her up by the waist and set her down gently. And every time he did it, she flinched just a little less. Then just as the sun began to lower towards the West he decided it was time to move on.

He stopped her and opened an ear pad again.

It seemed like hours, it must have been hours, since she had heard anything. She was starting to suffer auditory hallucinations and was sure she could hear birdsong. She had stood on the brinks of some cliffs – he had picked her up and carried her to the edges. She had been sure that was what they were. Her toes had curled over the edges of sun warned rock, and then from nowhere he had lifted her to safety. His arms were strong around her and she was safer than she had ever felt – but it was so brief. And then she was alone in the dark again.

And now he opened an ear pad and his voice was there, lightening the darkness, breaking the monotony.

"Leading a naked woman around for a day and more, gives a man appetites, Angel."

Her heart leaped with excitement. He wanted sex, he wanted sex with her. That would mean his body against hers, inside hers, warm and human. "But, you know," he went on, "a man like me needs more than just sex." Her heart sank. "I need to feel that you understand my right to cause you pain; to punish you if necessary. And *I* know that you need that as well. But do *you* know that?"

Angel nodded. Not because she agreed that he had the right to dominate her, to punish her, to do what he wanted with her, but because she needed his body.

He untied her wrists and raised them in front of her. She made no move to try and remove the hood or to run for it when they were free for a brief moment. In fact she wanted them held and secure once more. She felt a rope fastened to them and they were lifted until she was quite well stretched and standing on tip toe. She assumed she was tied to a tree branch. But it didn't really matter, and it didn't really matter if it was being done in front of an eager crowd.

Just so long as this quiet, infuriating, controlling man was there....

She felt something cold against the back of her ribs, he turned it slightly and in her state of heightened sensibility, she strained to understand the feeling he was trying to convey, and in her mind's eye she began to reconstruct the shape. It was a doubled over belt.

Even through the almost impermeable thickness of the hood she heard the smack it made. And she also felt the blow – like a punch. It nearly knocked the wind out of her and she swung forwards on the end of her rope, nearly falling and spinning as she did so. The next blow fell across her stomach and she spun again, yelling into the hood as the hot stinging spread across her front. Another blow caught her across one thigh and she lifted it up in instinctive defence. Then another landed on her buttocks and she arched backwards, spinning again to present her breasts. They were duly dealt with and inside her hood she yelled herself hoarse. No one had ever abused her this way. Always she had been fit and strong and been the predator. But now she hung and spun blindly, naked and vulnerable; desperate for the man who was beating her to take her.

It was only when it had gone on for a long time and she was sweating and gasping in the accursed hood, that she fully took on board that it didn't matter how much she wanted anything. She could yelp and howl and hope he would stop and fuck her. But he wouldn't; not until she accepted that he would only do it when it suited him to do it. With that realisation came calm and she endured her partial suspension, calves aching atrociously while the belt stung her back, her thighs and her belly again and again. The gasping and crying inside the hood were almost deafening and she was aching for him to touch her directly.

When he did she cried out even more loudly. The belt landed an especially spiteful blow to the tops of the backs of her thighs and with no warning, as she was still absorbing it, his hand was at her delta. His fingers drove between the thighs she had clenched against the pain of his last strike and brooked no resistance. She surrendered to him, realising what he wanted to feel and realising also that it was what she wanted him to feel. As far as she could she spread her thighs and his fingers slid down into a hot morass between her lips. The coarse skin of his finger tip sliding over her clitoris made her shiver with desire for him.

His fingers withdrew and she sobbed with desolation. For a few moments nothing happened and she blindly craned her head around seeking for any clue as to what came next. His naked warmth against her stinging hide was the next thing she felt and she nearly fainted with pleasure at the intimacy of the touch after so long in the dark. She felt his chest against her back and the hard rod of his cock bored between the cheeks of her arse, his fingers reached around and plunged down once more, this time almost lifting her off her feet and cradling her entire body in his strong, capable, cruel hands. He lifted her legs backwards and with one hand located himself at her vaginal entrance and thrust in. The ache in her arms was now terrible, she was being fucked from behind and her whole weight now was being taken by her arms. He made no more move to support her, just kneading her breasts and plunging in and out of her; taking his pleasure. To her own amazement she suddenly broke through into another new understanding. It was up to her how she coped with it. He was entitled to take from her whatever he could because she wanted him to. And with this understanding she was able to add the pain in her arms to the pain from the beating and somehow it all came together with the gathering ecstasy at her belly.

When she climaxed, it was with an intensity she hadn't experienced since Anne Lukins had first seduced her.

If she thought that her day was over when he cut her down and allowed her a few moments to recover, she was wrong. He fed the leash between her legs again and jerked it up with no lessening in his insistence. She scrambled up and was led off again.

This time it was to water again. He led her into it up to her ankles and then to her alarm, he dropped the lead, undid both ear pads and went. Frantically she cocked her head trying to find a trace of him.

"Do you trust me?" His voice came from some way ahead of her. "Then walk to me!"

Without a second thought she set off, if she fell into a pothole or was swept away, he would deal with it. Everything that concerned her was now his to do or not to do. She walked with confidence, hooded head held high. He wouldn't let her fall. And sure enough, suddenly she was in his arms.

"Tell me what Anne Lukins should have done," he said.

"Punished me! She should've done it to me. I wanted it so much! But I didn't understand, I wanted to be told I was bad. I wanted to be told I was good. And I wanted to be punished to make me know the difference."

"You've been good today," he told her and inside her hood she smiled. She was naked and beaten, oozing sperm down her thighs, but this was how he wanted her so this was how she wanted to be. It was all so simple now.

But even then there was more. He reached between her legs again and gathered up the leash. Her ears were sealed off once more and with no more than one encouraging tug she walked easily and confidently after him, until a heavy hand on her shoulder stopped her. She felt the leash drop and the ear pads were opened. A strong breeze rushed past her, she heard and felt it. And she felt, she really felt the height of the place where she was standing.

"Move forwards half a pace!" His voice came from her left. She did as she was ordered and nearly fell. The front part of her lead foot was over nothing. Cautiously she felt about until she had the edge located and then she stood with her toes curled over it. Her heart thundered. What would it be this time?

"Do you trust me Angel?" His voice was still over on her left, soft, she couldn't tell the distance. She nodded.

"Then take a step forwards."

Her heart stopped for a second.

And then she took the longest step of her life. Into the dark.

Angel lifted her right foot and paced forwards into nothingness. And was caught.

"Didn't I tell you I'd never let you fall!" His voice was close and in her darkness Angel laughed in pure delight.

The second night that they spent in the open, Angel, now freed of the hood but secure and happy in her collar and wrist cuffs, they camped round a fire he had built not more than ten feet away from where he had first ambushed her. He showed her the small outcrop that she had stepped off and how he had had to take no more than two steps to gather her up. Although had he not, she would have fallen all of four feet.

She fed happily from his hand and when it was dark he stood up and called for Ayesha. In just a few seconds she stepped into the clearing.

"Ayesha's always been mine," he told the bemused Angel. "I came here to claim her back and to claim you. She's walked in the dark with me as well, haven't you?" He turned back to where she knelt up in front of him and Angel didn't think she had ever seen a look of such joy on any woman's face. Gone was the distant, aloof expression that had been so familiar to anyone who had had dealings with her. Her bright-eyed, ecstatic calmness was more akin to the expression Blondie wore when Carlo was nearby. And now she could understand why.

She almost laughed aloud at the thought that the stereotypical reaction of two girls finding they were both entangled with one man was to have a catfight. But she felt nothing towards Ayesha now except a deep understanding. They were both lucky enough to belong to this man. He had allowed them to serve him and they would repay him with every breath they took.

He opened out two sleeping bags for them so they could sleep together and allowed them to keep their hands free so that they could get to know each other.

"You'll be spending a lot of time together from now on," he told them as he went to his own bag on the far side of the fire.

Angel immediately embraced Ayesha and kissed her deeply, savouring the feel of the heavy tongue ring as the slave's tongue explored her mouth. Her hands roamed over the smooth, toned flesh and found the hot little pit at her delta, moist and open.

"Angel!"

Lang's voice was soft but firm. He wanted her and she fumbled her way free of the bag and went to him.

He was lying on his bag and as she reached him he unzipped his trousers and pulled them and his pants down to mid-thigh. His cock lay semi-tumescent across one leg. It was plain that he needed some quickly administered relief and Angel crawled forwards and began to lick him into full erection. It was something she had never done before. The taste was strange, much more strong and earthy than the woman taste she was used to, but the skin was wonderfully soft. On the odd occasions that she had allowed a man access to her body, she had never felt any desire to investigate his cock. She had enjoyed a good struggle and a quick fuck, that was all, but here she knew she was pleasuring a man. Her man. Her Master, and his cock was the seat of the manhood that had shown her what she really was. Impatiently she shook her hair back and returned to licking the hardening shaft, instinctively she knew that a man wanted to see his woman worship his cock. And she did, slowly licking it to full, magnificent hardness. His helm seemed to dwarf her face, its round, gleaming fullness making her want to feel its smoothness on her tongue. She rounded her tongue and flicked it at the slit that traversed the head, exploring him and listening for his sighs of pleasure. Then at last she knew it was time. She opened her mouth as wide as she could, furling her lips across her teeth and sank slowly onto him. It was alarming at first. He filled her so completely that her tongue was flattened to the floor of her mouth as she ducked lower onto him and felt the massive helm lodge against the back of her throat. She almost gagged but managed to stop herself by relaxing and concentrating on his pleasure. Then she began the slow nodding motion she had seen slaves use on their masters, giving her own Master the feel of penetrating a tight and responsive vagina. She knew that at any moment he would start to come and although she wasn't certain she could get it all down she was determined to do her best and not to do anything that might inhibit his climax. She felt his hand on her head and he began to thrust into her mouth more forcibly. It was up to her how she dealt with the size of him and the excitement of that thought made her eager to receive the tangible evidence of his pleasure. Suddenly she felt the massive thing swell even more. Above her he gave a strained grunt and pushed her head further down onto himself, his huge helm lodged firmly in her throat and he began to come.

Angel had seen plenty of men coming; watching them wank over a well-whipped slave had always been something she had enjoyed, but nothing could have prepared her for the volume and force of the ejaculation in the narrow passage of her throat. Its slimy consistency and saltiness she immediately appreciated was going to be an acquired taste. And she so much wanted to acquire it. Desperately she tried to swallow but it was too much and despite her best intentions it went up her nose and she spluttered and choked as he splashed his come into her, time and again. She whined in disappointment as he softened and shrank and she tried to make amends by cleaning him as thoroughly as she could. Eventually he hauled her up by her hair and sent her back to bed. She could get no clue as to whether he was furious with her or whether he understood how disappointed she was with herself. Back in the warmth of the sleeping bag with Ayesha, she shared the taste of him with her before dropping into a deep sleep.

At mid morning they reached the house. Both girls trailed behind him, Ayesha on her tongue leash, Angel on the leash from her collar. Angel's eyes never left his hand, the hand that held the loop of her leash. With her hands clipped behind her and her lead held by him, nudity held no fears. She was safe.

Carlo and Ralph Lockhart came to the door and there was much hilarity at the fact that he had returned with two slaves, albeit it later than planned. There was some conversation about her, but it was none of her business and she ignored it, concentrating instead on the hand which held her lead. She only took an interest when she saw her master turn and look at the person who had just laid their hand on her buttock.

"You've done a job on this one, Mr Lang! I thought she was domme through and through!" It was Sara.

"She just needed a bit of tender loving care," her Master replied, smiling. "And now she needs hardening up to the whip and she'll be a nice little earner."

"You're going to put her into the arenas?"

"She's got the build."

"Hasn't she just!" The girl's hands were running over her breasts and down towards her crotch. Her master was making no move to stop her so Angel decided she must have some sort of right to do what she was doing.

"If you want me to start the hardening up process, just let me know," the girl said with a wicked chuckle.

"Why not? I've got to sort out payment for Ayesha. You could start on her right away if you'd like. She might as well get acquainted with the cane."

"Good choice. Break her to that and everything else will follow."

"True, so you might as well give it to her hard and get her broken in quickly. No point in spoiling the livestock."

Her master handed both leads to the girl and disappeared into the house. Clicking her tongue the girl led them round to the stables at the back. She handed Ayesha to one of the maids, ordering her to tie her up to one of the walls. Angel she led to the back of the yard and left her for a moment while she dragged a bench with a padded top and shackles on each leg out of a small room.

Angel's only emotion was curiosity. She had put countless girls over these things and thrashed them long and hard. Now she was going to find out what it was like, because her master wanted her to.

She spread her legs obediently to have her ankles chained and then bent forwards to lie across the sweat stained leather of the top. Her wrists were uncuffed and pulled down to be cuffed inside the more sturdy ones mounted on the bench legs.

Once she was mounted, Angel looked around her as best she could and saw the girl tying back her thick hair then stripping off her shirt and bra. She saw Angel watching and jiggled her breasts tauntingly.

"If you're very good, I'll ask Sir if you can suck them for me later!" she said and then picked up the cane. It was a long one with tape wound round one end. Angel knew that it was capable of really testing a girl and she was looking forward to it.

She looked straight ahead at the stones of the yard's wall and waited patiently while the girl teased her with flicks of the cane and quick forages with her fingers into her cunt.

"Hmm, quite wet! Mr Lang did do a good job on you. First time down for the cane they're usually pretty dry."

Angel knew that to be true, but then she was lucky. She knew her master wanted her caned.

The first full strength strike made her blink as she was knocked forwards. There was a second's numbness and then a blaze was lit in her haunches that brought tears flooding to her eyes. Then the second landed and the urge to scream was almost irresistible as the pain mounted to an intensity she had never dreamed existed. The third nearly broke her but then she realised that she would be looking beautiful even as she suffered. In her mind's eye she saw herself bent and spread legged, her buttocks rippling under the assault of the cane which was leaving its tramlines scoured across the smooth expanse of her arse. It was a familiar scene to her and she found it helped to visualise herself as anyone enjoying her caning would see her.

She bit down on the scream that the fourth made her want to let loose. She knew quite well that a slave making too much noise under the cane would spoil it for the master or mistress and she didn't want to do that after choking on his sperm the previous night. She took two more strokes with no more than explosive hisses of expelled breath and fidgeting with her feet.

There was a pause and the girl's hands explored her blazing hinds and made their way back into her cunt. Angel wasn't at all surprised to feel how easily she was penetrated, the thought of what she looked like under the beating had been very arousing.

The girl started in again after a few minutes and delivered another six hard lashes. Angel had almost gone beyond pain by then and was instead hoping that when he saw her, her master would be pleased.

After the twelfth lash she was left, sniffing and blinking to wait for whatever would come her way and to her joy she heard male voices and heavy shoes crossing the yard from the house.

She felt hands stroking her lines and bruises, then feeling her cunt and commenting on how wet she was and how well the marks suited her. But all the time she listened for her master and she felt she could take the cane all day when he said what a fine arse she had.

"But she's got a lot to learn," he added. "She can't suck cock to save her life."

"Practice makes perfect," Lockhart suggested.

"True. But I want her beaten a lot more as well."

Eventually it was decided that Lockhart's daughter should continue the lesson with the cane while the men would continue her lesson in cock sucking. After a bit of experimenting they found that if her wrist cuffs were moved up a hole on the front legs of the bench, her mouth was a reasonable height for their cocks. Once that had been found to be the case, the beating began again.

After the rest, the pain was even more intense and she couldn't help giving a scream as each lash bit into her. But it was alright, she heard her master say that she screamed quite prettily and in any case with a mouthful of cock, it wouldn't disturb anyone. One by one the men presented themselves at Angel's mouth and as she jerked and screamed her way through a bitterly harsh caning, she sucked at their cocks again and again until finally, despite the agony of the cane she managed to get an ejaculation down smoothly.

There was amused applause and the men went indoors for a pre-lunch drink, leaving Angel, heavily striped and bruised, dripping with sweat and sperm and deliriously happy.

CHAPTER EIGHTEEN

Carlo had brought the horse box up from The Lodge and so they travelled back in that. Angel's hired car was returned and Peter Lang travelled in the front with Carlo. In the back his two new possessions made themselves comfortable in their stalls.

The men took the driving in turns and came back for a blow job when they took a break. They used Angel's mouth exclusively, breaking her in to taking a man down smoothly. Ayesha just had to look on in envy as the thick shafts of cock stretched her mouth wide and then fucked her face. Once again she choked on the first couple of ejaculations and received the crop across her breasts as punishment. But by the end of the journey was achieving what Peter Lang considered an acceptable level of competence for a beginner.

Once back at CSL, Ayesha and Angel had to share a stall and they stayed for several days, long enough for Carlo to pierce Angel's tongue and for the ring to begin to settle in. Her master held her down, kneeling at the block while the deed was done and his hands, steady and commanding on her shoulders made the pain worthwhile. And the heavy ring rendering her almost mute made her feel evermore like her Master's creature and just like Ayesha.

The grooms adapted quickly to having Angel back on the premises as a slave, where once she had been a trainer. Patti was clearly itching to be allowed to play with her but no such order was forthcoming so the redhead beat anyone else who stepped out of line in the slightest until she was put to the whipping post in the yard herself by Tony, for having caned Eve far too hard for a slight misdemeanour.

The two girls found that as they were bedded down under one sheet, if they laid awake long enough to make sure all the others were asleep, their chains were long enough to allow one of them to wriggle herself upside down. And quietly they enjoyed leisurely sixty-nines, their noses jammed against the other's perineum, their tongues aching as they rasped them over the other's clitoris. They managed it for three nights but then fell asleep before they could return to their proper sleeping stations and were discovered by Raika in the morning.

Peter Lang tailored the punishment to fit the crime. In the training arena they were hung by their ankles back to back and with their hands clipped together behind their backs, only able to feel the other's buttocks.

Angel was mortified at how angry her Master was and ashamed of her self indulgence. Of course he was perfectly right; a slave had no right to pleasure herself without permission and the fact that the sleeping arrangements rather shoved temptation in their faces was neither here nor there.

In the morning they were beaten across their breasts and stomachs. Then in the afternoon they were hauled up again, having only been lowered to lie in a heap on the sand of the arena, and whipped between their legs.

Angel could only think of how much pleasure she had always taken in seeing a girl spread out for her as she was for her Master. She had loved the individual structure of each girl's cunt, the different ways the inner and outer lips, pouted, bloomed, quivered and opened as the whip fell. She had loved how the girls would cry out as the clit was struck. She had adored the long strike, going clear between the legs and landing along the arse crack.

Had the beating been for her master's pleasure she would gladly have taken every lash he wanted to give her. But it was a punishment and the pace was slow, allowing them to fully savour the pain of each lash without adding to it quickly enough to allow her to build her own pleasure.

Carlo stood one side and her Master the other, taking it in turns to lash them.

"If you want to make the beast with two backs, you can take your punishment as a beast of two fronts," he told them before the long afternoon began.

Patti led them back to the stables and she could have used the tongue leashes but chose instead to clip leashes to their bound wrists, run them forwards along their stinging and burning cunts and then heft the leads over her shoulder as she led them, hopping and yelping behind her.

They resisted temptation that night.

The following day Peter Lang ran them as a two in hand. They were matched in height and made a striking sight; blonde and black haired. He tacked then up for dressage with gold bracelets and chains at their wrists, beautifully crafted gold filigree bands at their upper arms and ankles. And bells at their breasts.

Ornamental golden nipple caps were placed on them, and gold spiralled out to crown the breast itself. From the tip of the nipple cover hung tiny bells that nevertheless had a carrying chime. The whole assembly was kept in place by a pin through the nipple. Ayehsa was clearly used to them and made no fuss but when her master tried to pierce her Angel she made such a fuss that Carlo had to hold her shoulders.

Once her tender flesh had given way to the steel and the pain had subsided to a nagging ache, Angel was thrilled at how the bells jingled when her master slapped her breasts and made them swing.

She had pierced many girls herself but now, as she listened to the bells chiming as she was walked to the cart she was to pull, she realised that she was the really lucky one. The piercer only got the pleasure of performing the act; the slave, however, continued to enjoy the pain and the pride of wearing her master's mark

She also soon discovered that running in harness with a dildo inside her whilst trying to co-ordinate her every movement with Ayesha's was not as easy as she had assumed. She didn't regret for one minute any of the whippings she had dealt out to girls that she felt were being recalcitrant or just stupid, she just appreciated the fact that her master needed to lash her as hard as he did and was delighted by his quiet words of approval when she managed to get her knee lift to match her partner's precisely. Learning to keep her blinkered head steadily facing forwards while she tried to absorb everything else that was being beaten into her was a task that she found a pleasing challenge. In the end she hardly noticed the ache at her nipples and the tinkling of the bells. But nevertheless she pranced and shied as the needles were withdrawn back at the stable while Ayesha was bent forwards over the crossbar of the cart and fucked by their master. She was grateful for the chance to kneel before him afterwards and lick his softening shaft clean.

Before she was returned to her stall Carlo and her master had her bend and touch her toes with her legs spread, being so blatantly exposed to so many eyes as the grooms went about their business, made her alert to what was being said about her. The discussion focussed on her backside, her buttocks still carried traces of the cane and the day's whipping and she felt her master's fingers trace their courses from hip to hip. But it was at the puckered crater of her anus that they stopped the most.

"She's tight as a duck's," she heard him tell Carlo and was immediately distraught at not being satisfactory for him.

"She probably only had the occasional strap-on up it from Sadia," Carlo said.

Angel wished she could help matters by explaining that Sadia had very rarely buggered her, preferring her cunt instead – although both of them had happily buggered the slaves often enough.

"I'll have to stretch it in due course. She'll be more responsive in harness when she's double plugged."

Angel just wished he would do it. If it would make her more pleasing to him.

"I've got a medium sized one I keep in case we ever get a tight one. Just shove it in and let her get used to it." Oh, please! She thought. Make me the way you want me.

"Tempting but we've got to be going tomorrow," her master said. "I've sorted out a flight for us." He slapped Angel's haunch and pulled her upright before handing her over to a groom. The last thing Angel heard as she was led away was that her master was taking her home and it was a mark of how deeply subservient she was to him now that she could face that with complete calmness, as long as he was with her.

Sadia had been left dumbstruck by Peter Lang's phone call. And two days later she still didn't really believe it. Angel enslaved? Not Angel! Not her cool, cruel Angel who dominated every slave in the place, who would happily have a girl strung up and whipped every day if that was what it took to bend her to her will.

But nevertheless she decided to play it carefully. Just in case he was telling the truth, she arranged for the truck picking him up from the airport to come directly to the main door of the house, thus bypassing the training ground. If Angel really was being delivered back in a CSL crate, it might not be good for the slaves' morale to see her.

When the truck's arrival was announced Sadia went to the front door with keen curiosity and even when she saw the two crates unloaded from under the tarpaulin on the back of the pick up, she had trouble believing her own eyes. Hog tied and travel stained it might be but there was no mistaking the blonde figure lying next to Ayesha.

Rather stunned, not sure how to react and unsure even about her own feelings towards Angel and Peter Lang, she shook his hand and invited him in.

"Have these two put in the cells by the playroom," she instructed the guards before following her guest indoors.

Over drinks in her office Peter explained how he had enslaved Sadia's erstwhile trainer and how he had also enslaved Ayesha.

"Well, Peter! You've given me some real problems here," she said when he had finished. "I have an empty space in my bed and a vacancy on my training staff with a home fixture only a matter of weeks away."

"I stopped off at CSL for a few days on my way here, as you recall I rang you from John Carpenter's office. I have a feeling that I might be able to assist you and repair some of the damage I've done the Girl Squad; damage that I greatly regret. However you must admit, Countess, that the prospect of having a properly subservient Angel at one's beck and call is a temptation that no one could resist!"

Sadia laughed. "I have to admit that I cannot hold that against you! She is a gorgeous creature."

"In talking with Carlo and Brian, it turned out that you have a slave here who used to work for CSL. I can't promise anything just yet but if you would give me a few minutes in here with her alone, we might find out that the solution to our problems is very close at hand."

Sadia's interest was immediately piqued; and not simply because of the need to appoint a new trainer urgently. Ninety-seven had made an impression way beyond what her status would have suggested she was capable of. The brutality of Angel's revenge was testimony in itself, so she happily left Peter alone in the office and had the girl summoned to him.

Once Amelia had been released from the sick bay and returned to the squad, she had once again been singled out for Angel's special treatment. With several weeks to go before the next games, it was quite proper to use a live target for whip drill. The only thing was that it was always Amelia who spun and yelped at the end of a rope as girl after girl was put through her paces to hone her speed and accuracy.

However, when Angel left it seemed as if the squad was just marking time. She had clearly not intended to be gone for more than a day or two and had left no orders concerning ongoing training. As the days went by and still she didn't reappear, some of the senior guards tried to organise a schedule of runs, sparring fights and assault course running, but the slaves themselves didn't put their hearts into it; even when the solitary pits were returned to full use. Sadia held several punishment sessions and wielded the lash herself but it just wasn't the same.

Freed of Angel's spite, Amelia had found herself increasingly angry with the whole set up. She fumed at the lack of discipline and drive, she wanted to be pushed to perform at her absolute limits, she wanted to face opponents on the training ground but what she increasingly found herself doing - after the games at the Orange stadium – was laying out in her mind what the Girl Squad ought to be doing. Who should be made to go on runs to slim them down a bit, which girls needed drilling in studded whip wielding, which of them needed pursuit running practice.

It wasn't what she had longed for. She had longed for total submission to the will of a trainer but now she had tasted the power a trainer had, she couldn't be at ease.

So it was with a depressed sort of indifference that Amelia followed the guard who had summoned her up to Sadia's office. To her surprise Sadia wasn't there and it took her a few moments to recall the rangy, tanned man who sat beside Sadia's desk. She had seen him at the Bakhtar arena and at some of the arena world gatherings and auctions.

"You know who I am?" he asked, standing up and approaching her. She nodded.

He seemed satisfied and turned to a battered leather bag on the floor, from which he took a sturdy leather hood.

"Sadia has given me permission to see if we can't break you of these ideas above your station that Angel has been complaining of," he told her as he came towards her with the hood held so it could be slipped over her head.

Amelia's patience finally snapped. If she was being indisciplined then it was Angel's or Sadia's job to whip her back into line. And if they couldn't do it then they didn't deserve to own a stable. She backed away but he was too agile and quick. A leather-scented darkness descended on her as sight and sound were utterly denied her under the thick padding. A draw string was pulled tight at her neck and the darkness and imprisonment was complete. For a second or two she snorted in panic through her nose as she realised that even her mouth was blocked, but once she had quietened down, she felt an ear pad being unzipped.

"Now, I'm going to clip a lead to your collar and you're going to walk with me in the dark." Lang's voice was close beside her and hardly had she registered his words than she was marooned in darkness and silence once more.

She felt a lead being clipped to her collar and tugged.

She resisted. Who did he think he was? Who did any of them think they were? She had come looking for the rigours of true submission and slavery – and now the stable was falling apart in front of her and they had had to bring in this man because they couldn't control her. Well to hell with all of them!

She felt the lead tugged harder and pulled back all the harder against it.

There was a burst of scarlet pain in her darkness as a riding crop snapped home across the backs of her thighs. She reared back and twisted. She wasn't going to go on any magical mystery tour! Already she was thinking of some way – any way - to regain her freedom.

There was another tug and Amelia planted her feet further apart and prepared to dig in. But to her surprise she felt the hood being loosened and slipped off.

To her even greater surprise, as she blinked her eyes in the light, she saw Peter Lang smiling broadly at her.

"I think we understand one another, Miss Johnson," he said and unclipped her lead as Sadia came in.

"Exactly as I thought," Lang told her. "Amelia here is ready to assume an entirely new role as trainer of the Girl Squad."

Sadia came to her and took her arm as her jaw dropped in the wake of Lang's announcement.

"Come and sit down and I'll explain," her owner told her.

An hour later, still trying to come to terms with the facts that Angel was now a slave and that she had been invited to take her place because she had refused to submit to Lang, Amelia's tongue ring was cut and removed.

"Like Angel," Lang told her afterwards, "you didn't fully understand your own nature. She had no idea she was really a submissive, you had no idea that you were a switch – able to dominate or submit. You've experienced total submission and were getting restless. Inside you something was telling you it was time to move on and you've got the makings of a superb trainer. After all, you'll be the only one on the circuit who's been out on the arena floor, taking everything that comes at you."

One of the female guards had found some clothes and with just a shirt and a short, linen skirt making her feel constrained and over-dressed, Amelia found herself sitting beside Sadia in her drawing room.

A lot of what Peter Lang said made sense, she had been feeling dissatisfied with herself and with the stable. She did have a lot of ideas about how things could be run better and she was uniquely qualified.

"But I think there'll be times when I'll need the other side of me let out and how will I be able to do that?" she asked, her voice still thick and her speech hesitant after so many months of being mute.

Sadia laid a hand on her knee. "I'll be more than willing to attend to that personally!" she assured her, looking deep into her eyes. "And we'll play with that lovely little friend of yours too. Then every now and again I'll take you to this charming club I'm a member of and they'll be able to satisfy absolutely any appetite at all! Trust me on this."

Amelia felt Sadia's hand tighten on her knee and got a stomach churning jolt of arousal as she considered being the lover of one of the owners.

"But what about Angel?" she asked, trying to get her feet back on the ground before lust swept her away.

"Mr Lang has very kindly given her to us, as well as Ayesha. Just think of it, Amelia! You'll have both of them to deploy as you want. And the best of it is, it'll still be the Girl Squad. Owned and trained by girls!"

"I don't intend to interfere at all, Amelia," Lang put in. "I shall do what I'm good at and will be out and about gathering information that might be useful to you and the stable. But I'll be in the background and I'll only need Ayesha and Angel on a personal basis from time to time and always with your permission being sought in advance."

Amelia looked around her and then got up and went to the window that looked out over the training ground and the barracks.

"I'll need to start attending some auctions for the new stock we need and a new barracks will be needed."

"It's all in hand," Sadia said coming to stand at her shoulder and putting an arm round her waist.

Amelia took a deep breath. "I want Angel put into all the barracks in turn for an hour tomorrow. She's to go in alone and all the slaves are to be free." She looked around her defiantly. "If she's to fight alongside them, they need to know she's really one of them. And the only way to do that....."

".....Is to let them knock seven bells out of her," Lang agreed. "And a few days in a solitary pit wouldn't hurt either."

Sadia raised a glass of champagne. "Here's to our new slaves and our new trainer!"

Amelia lifted her own glass. "And here's to the Girl Squad!" she said.

WHEN THE MASTER SPEAKS

by

Josephine Scott

Two women separated by a hundred years, but connected so intimately in other ways. Clarisse's letters recounting her experiences in nineteenth century London are linked with Lauren, a twentieth century woman. Clarisse's letters explicitly spell out her erotic adventures and in the house where so much took place, Lauren is herself bound up in the passionate ties of submission that link the two. An erotic classic.

BAD BLOOD

by

Sean O'Kane and Francine Whittaker

What starts as a trivial spat over a
boyfriend escalates into a full blown cat fight
between Vanessa and Rae.
Soon others are drawn into the consequences of
their enmity and the two young beauties are having
plans made for them that they know nothing about.
Powerful men are looking to profit from the bitter
squabble and the two girls are quickly led towards a
future neither of them could possibly have envisaged.
Bad Blood is a unique event in erotic publishing,
combining as it does the talents of a submissive
authoress and a dominant author. The result is a truly
explosive read!

THE STORY OF EMMA

By

Sean O'Kane

A bundle of diary entries and jottings that arrived at the Silver Moon offices and which were forwarded to Sean O'Kane have provided erotic fiction with one of its most remarkable heroines.

Emma Stewart – a smart self-confident and professional young woman recounts how she came under the spell of the BDSM world. With complete honesty she brings the reader into her life as she struggles with balancing her profession against her sexuality. Something has to give!

And as Emma is drawn ever more deeply into the world of submission and dominance, she encounters enemies from her former life who are determined that she will pay for her conduct. Working from Emma's own notes and jottings, Sean describes her downward path in searingly erotic detail to the point where her two worlds collide – painfully!

Emma is the most memorable heroine since O herself!

Membership of the Silver Moon readers' club is absolutely free!

You can order copies of Silver Moon, Silver Mink and Silver Mistress books from the privacy of your own home. And you can also pre-order new publications and receive a substantial discount!

There are always offers for members and you can receive books that aren't on offer in any bookshops like some of our illustrated books.

Just cut out this page and send it to;
Silver Moon Reader Services,
Suite 7, Mayden House,
Long Bennington Business Park,
Newark NG23 5DJ

Don't forget to include your own name and address and you'll receive our latest brochure and an order form, plus you'll get £3.00 off your first order!

Over the coming months you'll get reviews of books from other readers, be able to exchange letters with the editor, read interviews with your favourite authors and lots more!

Membership is free and your privacy is assured.